Speculative North
Science Fiction, Fantasy, and Horror

Published by *TDotSpec Inc.*

Speculative North:
Science Fiction, Fantasy, and Horror

This is a work of fiction. The stories are products of their respective author's imagination and are not intended to be construed as real. Any resemblance to actual persons, living or dead, is entirely coincidental.

Cover Illustration by Eran Fowler
Published by TDotSpec Inc.

Copyright Acknowledgements:

"Noctua Steal the Moon" Cover Illustration Copyright © 2016 Eran Fowler
"Introduction" Copyright © 2020 David F. Shultz
"Autumn in the Dying Light" Copyright © 2020 Brian Koukol
"Bang the Drum" Copyright © 2020 Andy Dibble
"The Vulture Man" Copyright © 2020 Kai Calo
"The Air Show" Copyright © 2015, 2020 Rudy Kremberg
"The Heron King" Copyright © 2020 Eric Lewis
"The Laffun Head" Copyright © 2020 Christi Nogle
"Sullied Flesh" Copyright © 2020 Karl Dandenell
"The Selkie Wife" Copyright © 2020 Marcie Lynn Tentchoff
"The Edge of Galaxy NGC 4013" Copyright © 2020 Warren Brown
"After Dinner Conversation: An Interview With Publisher Kolby Granville" Copyright © 2020 David F. Shultz and Kolby Granville
"Craft: The Narrative Lens" Copyright © 2020 David F. Shultz

Speculative North Team

Lead Editor
David F. Shultz

Fiction Editor and Managing Editor
Don Miasek

Poetry Editor
W. T. Anderson

Copy Editor
Justin Dill

Marketing & Operations
Mitchell "the itch" Harris

Social Media Lead
K. M. McKenzie

Submissions Editors

A.M. Todd
Anna P.L.
Brandon Butler
Calder Hutchinson
Christina Fanciullo
Don Miasek
Emil Terziev
Gregg Chamberlain
Ian Mah

Jeff Butler
Jeremiah Kleckner
Jessica Rust
Justin Dill
K. M. McKenzie
Lisa Cai
Luc Moreau
Marlaina Stocco
Marty Hoefkes

Mitchell Harris
Paul Jarvey
Shivani Kamdar
Tommy Blanchard
Vineet Bhalla
Wayne Cusack
Y.M. Pang

Publisher
TDotSpec Inc.

Project Backers

We would like to extend a huge thank you to all of our project backers, without whose generosity *Speculative North* would not have been possible.

A. M. Todd
Annelise Knoot
Barbara Campbell
Bart Vervaet
Bryan Dawe
Cat Girczyc
Catherine Oyiliagu
Dan Allen
Daniel Merritt
David Perlmutter
Ed Rockwell
Emil Pellim
Eric Jepson
EssentialEdits.ca
Ian Chung
Irena K.

J Kyle Kelsey
James Downe
Jeffrey R. Butler
Kim Lightle
Lawrence Marzari
Lisa Cai
Margret Treiber
Maria Haskins
Mark Carter
Marlaina Stocco
Martin Munks
Michael Luscombe
Michael Weckworth
Mike Rimar
Nancy Kay Clark

Natalie Garceau
Pauline Lim
Peter G. Reynolds
Peter Hargraves
Peter Vroomen
R. Graeme Cameron
Rahul Bhagat
Randal Heide
Rob Petrungaro
Scott Thrower
Sean W. Scully
Stephanie A.
Suzanne Barcza
Wendy L Schultz

Lifetime Subscribers

We would like to thank the following supporters, who believed in our mission enough to become life-time subscribers to *Speculative North*.

/amqueue

Ellen Michelle

Joshua Lee Cooper

Kumsal Obuz

Jean Pierre Targete

Richard Ohnemus

Robbin Webb

Thomas Bull

Calder Hutchinson

Dimitri Sirenko

Top Backer

A super-special thank you goes out to our top supporter, whose generous donation funded an entire issue of *Speculative North*!

Anthony Nijssen

Introduction to Issue #3
David F. Shultz

The first two issues of *Speculative North* have been a fantastic success! Both issues hit Amazon #1 Bestseller status, we surpassed our distribution goal of 500+ readers for each issue, both issues continue to receive great reviews on Amazon and Good Reads, and both issues have received wonderful reviews from CSFFA hall-of-famer R. Graeme Cameron (these reviews can be found on *AmazingStories.com*). I would like to say thanks to all of our readers and reviewers—it is awesome to see all the positive reactions!

As in previous issues, the composition of issue #3 reflects our mission to be a diverse publication. This mission includes not only being a platform for speculative fiction that portrays the lives of minority populations, such as how Brian Koukol describes the everyday challenges a person with limited mobility may face in the near future in his "Autumn in the Dying Light." It also includes fresh ideas, such as Karl Dandenell's vision of future theater appreciation in "Sullied Flesh" and unique writing styles and cultures like those of Andy Dibble's "Bang the Drum."

This issue includes two poems and seven stories, including at least one in each of the genres of science fiction, fantasy, and horror. The amazing cover art comes from British Columbia artist Eran Fowler, who also created the cover art for our inaugural issue. The image suits the issue well, as motifs of birds and flight repeat throughout the issue. Issue #3 is dark, with several stories contending with themes of death, dying, and grieving. Other key themes and ideas include virtual reality, karma and Buddhism, and the afterlife.

One of our issue #3 stories is by a first-time published author, and four of our authors self-identify as writing from a historically marginalized perspective or identity. Representing diversity in stories, styles, and perspectives is critical to our editorial goals, and we're proud to achieve this in all our issues.

It should be noted that we do not select stories on the basis of author identity—this information is not used during the reading, reviewing, and voting process, but only to distribute stories in upcoming issues and make sure we are reaching our targets. For more information about our selection process and our editorial stance about diversity, please check out the introduction to issue #2, which is available free from tdotspec.com in digital magazine format, and from Amazon in paperback and kindle eBook format.

It's also been great to hear from submitting authors and to see the reputation that *Speculative North* is developing on social media. Many authors have reached out to thank our team for the feedback. On Facebook, Twitter, and Instagram, writers are endorsing *Speculative North* and suggesting that other authors submit. One of our goals is promoting and supporting the speculative community, so it's encouraging to see that we are having a positive impact and that authors appreciate what we're doing.

So far, we have maintained a 100% personalized feedback rate. Of course this is only possible because of the efforts of our reading team, who not only read and judge the stories, but also provide detailed written feedback. Our reading team for issues #1 through #5 comprises about 30 volunteers, who collectively read and review every submission at least twice. The diversity of perspectives and editorial tastes on the team is essential to our process, and it translates to greatly varied stories and styles in any given issue. Thanks, reading team, for all your hard work, insightful readings, and thoughtful reviews! I'd also like to specially thank our two unofficial super readers, who read and reviewed over a quarter-million words each so far! All feedback from the reading team is compiled and sent to authors in personalized letters. This critical and time-consuming job is mostly the work of our managing editor Don Miasek. Thanks Don!

It's great to see the growth of *Speculative North* and the enthusiastic response from authors and readers. I am excited about the future of this new literary community, and I hope you continue to be a part of it. If you like what we're doing with *Speculative North*, the best way to support us is to keeping reading future issues! According to our publishing model (explained in the issue #1 introduction), our back issues will always be free to anyone from our website. Sales are great, but it's more important to us that we put our authors' work in front of as many readers as possible. If you like any of the stories, please let the writers know in a review—it will really make their day!

Thanks so much for being a reader, and enjoy issue #3 of *Speculative North*!

—David

Contents

Autumn in the Dying Light
Brian Koukol

A cold rain curtained the covered walkway as Tom gripped the ball of his joystick, weaving his power wheelchair between the asses of his fellow students en route to Algebra II. He slowed as the asses—invading his seated eyeline as usual—bunched up at the top of an impassable set of stairs and spilled over without recognition of their miraculous feat. At the bottom of the steps lay his math class—so close, yet so far.

Tom veered to his left, cutting across the anonymous social current toward a sheet of rainwater that cascaded from the eave in front of him. He bowed his head and held his breath as he pushed through, wondering exactly how much rehydrated bird crap the frigid water had collected from the roof above.

Out in the open now, the wind carried the heavy mist directly into his face, pelting him with what felt like a million frozen butterfly needles. By the time he reached the isolated ramp that descended to the level of his math class, the vintage Members Only jacket he'd inherited from his dead grandpa had already soaked through.

At the base of the ramp, he once again injected himself into the bloodstream of the student body, slipping into the open-air corridor between commissary stalls that still stank of the greasy chocolate chip cookies baked earlier that morning.

His stomach grumbled against a distinct lack of breakfast, then iced over as he picked out the predatory face of Adam Adjamian from the oncoming crowd. Fortunately, Adam seemed more interested in pushing through the rain than in messing with him for once, but Tom still tried his best to blend in with the crowd, all too aware of the futility of such an act.

He clung tight to the ass in front of him and breathed a sigh of relief when Adam walked past without appearing to notice him. Scarcely had Tom's breath vanished into the misty drizzle, however, when his chair lurched to an unexpected halt. His seatbelt caught him at the waist and he managed to hold onto the binder on his lap, but the Algebra book stacked on top crashed to the wet ground, spilling the homework tucked inside.

The reptilian hiss of Adam's laugh sliced through the mist behind him.

"Hey, peeping Tommy," came the expected whisper in his ear. "Enjoy your bath. Too bad it won't wash the retard off you."

Tom tried to turn to confront his bully, but his motors refused to cooperate. He didn't know the engineer who designed the impossible-to-reach emergency killswitch on the back of his chair or how Adam had first discovered it, but he wished the Bible were real so they could both burn in hell.

Adam splashed through the pooling water as he ran off, leaving a helpless Tom to watch as his homework paper puckered in the downpour, the painstaking scratches of erasable pen blurring into something even less comprehensible than parabolic foci and directrices.

Stranded and saturated in rain, Tom scanned the crowd, looking for a friendly face, but found only strangers with their heads bowed against the weather.

He had a voice. He was more than capable of shouting for help. But he didn't, cowed by the fact that to ask for help was to admit weakness and the certainty that weakness was death. As the only mainstreamed gimp in his entire high school, he had to be stronger than everyone else. If he asked for help, the whole thing would fall apart.

Or maybe he was just embarrassed.

Tears filled Tom's eyes and tumbled from his cheeks, invisible in the downpour in a way he could never be to polite society. He was an imposter, trying to fit in where he so clearly didn't belong.

So there he sat. In the rain. Crying.

And then she appeared.

Nesrine Bahar. His wild rose. The only one who was more than an ass. Much more.

Like always, he saw Nessie's eyebrows first—dark, ponderous thickets that had no interest in tweezers or submission of any kind. She wore no makeup, nor did she need any. Not with eyes of an electric amber so vibrant and scintillating as to recall honey flecked in gold, even under such gloomy skies.

She nodded at him as she approached, then stopped with a frown. Her trademark army jacket hung at mid-thigh over black denim and combat boots the color of pig's blood.

"You okay, Tom?"

"Fine," he replied, rain and tears running from his chin. "Just enjoying the beautiful day."

She laughed and he could've sworn the sound steamed him completely dry. "You're crazy."

"Good thing too, or you wouldn't be able to stand me."

"True." She motioned to the math book at his feet. "That yours?"

His predicament felt like failure, and that wasn't the image he wanted to present to Nessie. She wasn't one for weakness.

"No," he said.

She shot him a skeptical glance and snatched his sodden homework from the ground. "It's got your name on it..."

He flushed. She probably wasn't one for liars either. "Oh, that one. Yeah, it's mine."

Nessie slipped the paper back in the book and brushed the water off its cover before returning it to his lap.

"You sure you're okay?" she asked.

"Yeah. See you in English?"

"Wouldn't miss it," she said with a smile he hoped she saved just for him. "One more unexcused absence and its Saturday school for me."

And then she was gone, abandoning him to the drizzle.

The bell rang.

The crowd thinned.

The rain intensified.

Tom's wet clothes itched against his shivering skin.

He shook his head, uncertain whether his current predicament was more Adam's fault or his own.

End program.

•

Tom deflated into consciousness with a hypnic jerk. His body slumped. His chest wall collapsed. Air hunger squeezed him from temple to sacrum. A condom catheter stung the margins of his abraded penis.

Straining against the chest belt of his wheelchair, he tucked his chin and took a sip from the mouthpiece of his ventilator after too long without. His torso rose with the assisted breath, straining against the constricted anatomy of his upper back. He exhaled it with a derisive chuckle of self-deprecation. If only his high school self had known how bad things would get in the future, maybe he wouldn't have taken easy breaths and covert masturbations for granted. Maybe he would've asked Nessie out. Maybe he would've made something of his life before it was too late.

With a sharp twist of his head, Tom forced free the cable that connected the MuninnDrive implanted behind his right ear to the antiquated desktop computer before him. The brain-side of the cable fell to the ground, but it didn't bother him. He'd have Myrna swab it with alcohol later.

Most Editors connected wirelessly to wearable, bleeding-edge MuninnDrives for the constructions and duplications of their memory edits, but Tom wasn't like most Editors. His MD, now 20 years past obsolescence, was a first-gen hard implant that his parents had only managed to afford by piggybacking onto his teenage spinal fusion surgery. Fortunately for Tom, modern MDs glossed over their edits with a warm nostalgic glow that his clientele didn't appreciate, favoring the cold reality of his vintage hardware instead. They also preferred the breadcrumb-free hardcopies his setup could provide that the ubiquitous cloud-uploads could not, which suited his purposes just fine. Paper trails meant reported income and reported income of anything approaching a living wage endangered his health benefits.

The edit he'd just finished duping, "Tears in the Rain," had been one of his first experimentations with the record function of his MD. It was also one of his most reliable moneymakers, despite being cut long before he'd learned the way intentional thought could give context to his work. Customers assured him it was the perfect way to dip a toe in misery porn, which had become his specialty. He was more than willing to share the pratfalls of his increasing debilitation with interested parties for the right price. They used his edits to make themselves feel better about their own circumstances after experiencing his, which he found hilarious since he himself used them as a ticket to the good old days when he could feed himself and pick his own nose and not obsess over the level of carbon dioxide in his blood. Perspective was a funny thing.

"Laundry or dishes?" Myrna shouted from the other side of the half-open curtain that separated his bedroom/office from the rest of his subsidized studio apartment. At least he registered it as a shout; two hundred fifty-eight square feet made even whispers loud.

Tom took another sip from his mouthpiece and pushed past the curtain with a quick manipulation of his thumbstick controller. "What do you mean?"

"It's the end of the month," Myrna said from her spot in the kitchenette, dressed as always in cartoon character scrubs. "If you want to make it to December, we've got to be careful with your hours. You plan on going to bed tonight, don't you? Then pick: laundry or dishes?"

"What about breakfast?"

"Already on the table," she said.

Sure enough, a divided tray of brightly colored pastes sat on his feeder, its robotic arms awaiting the verbal cue to shovel a manufacturer-guaranteed 92% of the so-called food into his mouth without incident.

"Laundry," he said, pulling up to the diminutive table.

Myrna disappeared behind his bedroom curtain in four strides. "Only the one edit going out today?" she asked.

"Yeah."

"You checked it?"

"Of course. Looks good."

Myrna stepped out from his bedroom with an armful of ripe clothes and the full data card. "Address?"

"I flicked it to you."

She shoved the card in her back pocket and pulled out her phone. "Got it," she said, then frowned. "If you're gonna keep sending me clear across town, I'm gonna have to raise my fee."

Ignoring her, Tom looked down at his breakfast pastes and took a deep sip on his ventilator. "Okay, Seymour," he said. "Feed me."

The feeder kicked into action with a squeak and a puff, selecting process yellow for the amuse-bouche. It was supposed to be paella, but it tasted more like potato starch and latex.

"This is food, right?" he asked as Myrna stuffed his dirty

clothes into the combo washer/dryer beneath the counter of the kitchenette. "You didn't heat up a paint palette by mis—" Seymour shut him up with another spoonful of slop.

"Seymour, stop," Tom said through his mouthful. When the machine scooped up some orange from an adjacent section instead, Tom swallowed his food and tried again, narrowly saving himself from the butternut squash ravioli in brown butter and sage sauce that tasted more like savory sherbet with kelp.

He turned his chair so he could reach his metal drinking straw, but hesitated at the sight of it. Like the world's most disgusting core sample, it told the story of his last half-dozen meals in rainbow layers of food-tainted skin cells, from the garnet of last night's alleged pasta puttanesca all the way back to the rose-scented Punjabi rice pudding of three breakfasts ago.

He looked over towards Myrna, already pulling her jacket on to leave. "Can you clean my straw before you go?"

"You want to eat lunch?"

"Of course."

She finished buttoning up her coat. "Then let me go. I'm already late for my ten o'clock."

"It'll take thirty seconds..."

Myrna opened the front door.

Tom sighed, emptying what little air remained in his lungs. He could probably cut a profitable edit from the situation, but he really didn't feel like wrapping his lips around the disgusting straw at the moment. "I'll make it worth your while..."

Myrna turned to face him, the annoying hint of a smile on her face. "What are you offering?"

"Senior year of high school. I shit my pants in art class. A girl nearby asked what smelled like rotting pumpkins. I call it—"

"Pass," she said. "Nobody wants your fecals, dude. I could shit myself right now if I wanted to. For free."

"Then what do you want?" he asked, already knowing the answer.

"I'd take some quality IP."

Inspiration porn. It chapped his ass to peddle in the stuff, but it served a much larger audience than his favored MP. People really seemed to get off on watching cripples improbably overcome adversity. It served the same basic purpose as misery porn, but in a more palatable form. More dishonest, too.

"Okay," Tom said.

Seymour kicked into action at the misinterpreted trigger word and shoved the spoonful of savory sherbet into his mouth. Tom swallowed it as quickly as he could, stopped the renegade robot with the proper phrase, and turned his attention back to Myrna.

"I've got one I call 'Courage in Adversity,'" he said. "Or is it 'Games without Frontiers'? Well, whatever. It's a new edit of some old footage. Follows me as I make the jump from adaptive PE to regular PE and then score a touchdown against Adam Adjamian in a flag football game."

Myrna crossed her arms. "The market for this vintage stuff is thinning out. Haven't you done anything inspirational since high school?"

"Not unless you count surviving."

She laughed. "Didn't you hear? Life's a death sentence.

Nobody survives."

"Maybe I'm friends with the governor..."

"Not in this dump you aren't."

"Touché. So do you want it or not?"

She cracked one of her knuckles. "Yeah. I'll take it."

"The master's worth five hundred, easy, and that's way too much for a straw-washing. One play. That's all you get."

"Nobody buys singles anymore. Five plays, or I won't be able to move it."

"Three."

"Deal."

After Myrna left, Tom leaned around his mouthpiece and sipped dirty water through his clean metal straw to calm his nerves. The first few minutes alone were always the toughest, bringing to life the lump of frigid fears that lived behind his sternum.

He cursed his flimsy government health insurance for the inadequate number of home health hours it provided. There was only one solution for him—robot help. Prices had dropped enough that the government was willing to replace human care with that of the bare-bones machine variety, providing an exorbitant co-pay was met without somehow setting off earned-income alarm bells.

To Tom, the idea was nearly utopian—24/7 assistance without the risk of no-shows and side hustles and forced human interaction. When he'd first learned of such an option, the business he'd begun as a means to stay housed and fed had taken on a new urgency. And now here he was, ten years later, one big under-the-table score from achieving his goal.

The food on the tray in front of him had already begun to oxidize, browning and congealing at its edges. Still, he had to eat.

"Okay, Seymour. Feed me."

The feeder kicked into motion with the usual puffs and squeaks, dipping once again into the savory sherbet with kelp, but got hung up halfway to Tom's mouth. He drove a bit closer to the table and rocked against his chest belt until he could reach the spoon. After slurping off the food, he grabbed the spoon with his teeth and tugged.

Seymour lurched back into action, delivering Tom an empty mouthful. He took it, of course, since the damn thing wouldn't continue until he did. It selected cyan for the next bite, running some disgruntled programmer's masochistic algorithm, but once again hung up, this time even further from Tom's mouth.

He tried to ease his way forward in pursuit of the spoon, but slipped on a wet and anxious thumb. His chair lurched forward in response and the ventilator mouthpiece arm smashed against the edge of the table, driving the mouthpiece under his chin and tight against his larynx—well out of reach.

Panicking, he spun from the table as a convulsion of excited nerves electrified his body. He sped toward the front door reflexively, inadvertently running into a wayward pair of socks. His front tire bounced over the unexpected obstruction, knocking his thumb from the joystick and the rest of his hand over the front of the platform that supported it.

He flexed his shoulder, his forearm, his back—anything to coax his gnarled fingers back into place—but his muscles were too far gone.

He was trapped, and in far worse a manner than Adam Adjamian had ever managed. There were no students within earshot here, no Nessie to happen upon him, no sympathetic proctor to eventually discover him. Regardless of how miserable he'd been, trapped on that rainy day in high school, there'd been no chance of dying from it. The situation he found himself in now couldn't have been more different.

To Tom's surprise, he spotted a pedestrian through the door-adjacent window, navigating the pathway that crossed in front of his apartment. He tried to shout at them, but they continued past, unable to hear such a feeble voice even through a window with a blown seal. He opened and closed his mouth, trying to get his chin behind the ventilator mouthpiece so he could wrap his lips around it and gain enough air to create a serviceable shout, but to no avail.

He tried to calm himself, breathing what little he could—in through his nose and out through his mouth. He wasn't suffocating yet. It was only panic. He still had ten minutes or so before his oxygen saturation dropped below the all-important 95% mark and started giving him major symptoms. He still had time to save himself.

Or to suffer a protracted and terrifying death.

"Seymour," Tom said, trying to remember the correct command for the feeder's redundant safety system through his jangled nerves. "Dial emergency services."

Seymour puffed, lurching into action. "Please enjoy your food."

"Dammit, Seymour. Help me. Dial emergency services. I'm in trouble."

"Please enjoy your food."

The damn thing was caught in a loop. Until it dispensed its spoonful, it wouldn't accept new commands.

He sought out the desktop computer in his bedroom niche, but it hid around the corner, its gaze tracker well out of range. The SmartPartment suite was his only hope.

"Apartment. Call 911. Please."

"I'm sorry," a tinny speaker intoned. "This account has exceeded its emergency credits for the current monthly cycle. Please try again later."

Tom tried to scream, but his diaphragm wouldn't cooperate. He imagined Myrna's lunchtime return and subsequent discovery of his dead body. Not that she'd know he was dead at first, propped in place by chest belt and armrest in much the usual position.

Terror swept across him in a staccato of fits and starts, the flashes of calm quickly surrendering to the sense that his body had turned to fissured crystals primed to collapse into dust. He tried to imagine nothingness, but found he wasn't equipped for it, his every attempt thwarted by the hypnic jerk not of a return from memory, but the dread of a permanent consignment to it. He'd leave nothing behind but a Möbius strip of medical expenses and whatever scattered digital trail of decontextualized misery and inspiration those pesky data hackers had lifted over the years.

Tom begged the window to deliver him another passerby and cursed its intransigence when it refused. He yearned for his high school body and fingers with the strength to crawl their way back to his thumbstick. He strained his atrophied muscles, trying anyway, imploring his sense memory to forget its debilitation for a split-second and cooperate for once, but the belt of air hunger cinched another notch tighter around his chest instead, counting down toward oblivion one crushing hole at a time.

The world receded into a blur. He stilled muscles quivering with adrenaline and pressed his tongue as hard as he could against the roof of his mouth, trying to pause time. As a snapshot, he could live forever, or at least until Myrna returned for lunch.

For an instant, he thought of accessing his MD. He'd downloaded its cache to the desktop the night before, as always, but everything that had happened since was still local. He could relive the experience of Myrna getting him up this morning instead of his current predicament, drifting off toward death unknown to himself. Or, better yet, he could relive the memory he'd been reliving earlier, spending his last moments with Nessie, fulfilled and euphoric while trapped in the biting cold rain.

Trapped.

The word brought him back to himself. No. He wouldn't give up. He couldn't. Not ever. He gulped for air, thrusting his head backward to try to open his chest, sucking as hard as he could.

The window resolved before him, stepping forth from the surrounding blur. Tom stared at the pathway and listened to the bleat involuntarily emanating from his throat. There should be somebody out there. A hero, come to rescue him at the last possible moment. That's how good stories worked.

He fought the impossible urge to tear open his chest belt, his shirt, his rib cage. Anything to give his lungs more room to expand.

Pinpricks of excited paisley carved erratic paths across his vision, but still he kept his eyes locked on the other side of the window, willing a Messiah to appear and deliver him from the insatiable grasp of doom.

A large ball of the juddering paisley congealed at the edge of his vision and tumbled toward center. No. Not paisley. Something with legs. Two of them, working in tandem to propel a man in a houndstooth blazer across the pathway in front of his apartment.

"Help!" Tom called, his attempted shout reminiscent of the bark of a toy poodle he'd once known that had been robbed of its vocal cords.

As was inevitable, the man continued out of sight. Tears stuffed Tom's nose, making it even harder to breathe. All was lost. He was going to die. Foolishly.

He ground his larynx against the ventilator mouthpiece, biting the air, hoping against hope to snag the rigid plastic with his teeth, but without success. He flexed his thumb. A solitary inch stood between it and full freedom of movement. That's all— one stinking inch between life and death.

And then he was back—the man in the houndstooth blazer, scurrying down the pathway toward Tom's door. Against all the odds, he must've heard Tom's call.

"Help!" Tom said again, managing even less volume than the last time.

His Savior scrambled up to the door and turned the handle,

but it didn't budge. Locked.

Tom resisted the urge to curse Myrna. Out of air to speak, he mouthed the word, "Pot."

His heroic rescuer squinted at him for a second, then dropped to the empty flowerpot on the other side of the window. When he rose, Tom heard the key in the lock and watched the deadbolt turn.

The door swung open, revealing his salvation in a beaming smile.

"Mouthpiece," Tom managed, gasping.

"What?" his grinning rescuer said.

"Below. My chin. Pull it. Forward."

"This?" The man asked, grabbing the ventilator mouthpiece arm pinned against Tom's throat.

When he nodded, the man jerked it forward an inch or two and Tom eagerly wrapped his lips around it, filling his lungs with a rush of cold room air. He knew it would take a while to return to himself, but, more importantly, he knew he'd been delivered by this handsome stranger.

"You saved. Me," Tom said between ravenous sips of air. "I thought. I was. Gonna die. If you. Weren't here. I would've. Bless you."

"Think nothing of it," the man replied, pressing his fists to his hips and raising his chin. "I'm always eager to help. In fact, it is I who should be thanking you!"

Tom tried his best not to cringe. "Why's that?"

The man raised his chin higher. "For allowing me to fulfill my life's purpose. Lending aid to those less fortunate than I!"

Tom took a few more breaths. He could already feel his hunger for air slake. The dull pain of relaxing muscles gripped his body, but was no match for the feeling of profound gratitude he felt toward this man.

He glanced up at the magnificent visage of his rescuer. "Can you help me get my. Hand back on the controller?" he asked.

The man broke from his pose. "Gladly." He frowned. "It looks like it's already there."

"Not quite. Can you move my thumb. Back an inch?"

"An inch? That's not much…"

"In a world of millimeters. An inch is plenty."

The man did as he asked and Tom took control of his wheelchair once again. A washed-out and disconnected world leapt to vivid life as he turned his chair in a tight circle. "How can I ever thank you?" he said.

The man's face contorted into a scowl of disappointment. "I'm not feeling it."

"Not feeling what?"

"The inch thing. I don't believe you were really stuck."

Tom shook his head to shed a tear of relief pooling in his eye. "Well, I was."

The man crossed his arms. "Just be warned, I'm not paying for—" he paled. "Oh God. I just messed it up, didn't I? I broke meta!"

"It's okay," Tom said. "I can edit it out later."

"Really?"

"Really. I've been doing this for a long time."

Color returned to his client's face. "Oh, thank God. I'd hate to have to go through that all over again. I'm double parked, you know? Anyway, while we've got this little moment here, how was it?"

"Great," Tom said, wishing Myrna would hurry up and get back so he could take a pain pill.

"Did you really think you were going to die? For real?"

"Yeah. For a while there, I did. I couldn't really think about it in the moment for the sake of immersion. But somewhere in the back of my mind I started to wonder if you were actually going to show up or if I'd just done something epically foolish."

The man grinned. "I came late on purpose. And then I pretended to walk past. I thought it might help the realism."

"Oh, it definitely did," Tom said. If he hadn't needed this big score to afford the co-pay on that home health robot, he might've rammed the fucker at full speed.

The man rubbed his hands together. "Great. And did you think about the insatiable grasp of doom like I told you?"

Tom closed his eyes, trying not to think about how close he'd just come to killing himself in pursuit of an amazing edit. It was probably the most courageous thing he'd ever done. "Sure did," he said.

"And you pondered the immensity of the void?"

"You bet. I pondered the shit out of it."

The man raised up onto his toes and then rocked back to his heels. "I can't wait to see it. I brought an external to make sure it's legit, but the real fun will come when I load it in my vintage MD back home. You're running a first-gen, right?"

"I am. As advertised."

The man returned to his earlier position, with hands on hips and elevated chin. "Okay, enough shop talk," he said. "I could go on all day and I'm sure you could too, but I want to finish this so I can enjoy. You may resume your adulation."

Tom held his tongue, a task made easier by the giddiness bubbling within himself at the thought of a goal accomplished. Ten years of saving and he'd finally pocketed enough coin to meet the co-pay of that home health robot. He could almost taste his future independence. No more rushing and worrying. He could finally relax.

After a lifetime of hurtling ever downward, things were finally looking up. After merely existing for thirty-four years, it was finally time for him to live.

End program.

•

The food pump whirred in a rhythmic reptilian whisper, pushing its milky beige nutrition through the gastronomy tube into Tom's stomach. A rush of air stung his tracheostomy stoma, forcing its way into his lungs with the immutability of the ocean's tides. He shifted his weight from a budding pressure sore and winced when his in-dwelling Foley catheter pinched the inside of his prostate gland.

Unable to turn his head with it strapped to his headrest, Tom pivoted his chair with a flick of his fingertip controller and rolled his gaze to the home health robot leaning against the corner of his bedroom niche. One of its plastic eyelids sagged halfway shut; the other showed nothing but the stark whiteness of sclera glass.

"Fuck you, Elemiah," Tom said to it through the valve that allowed him to speak while ventilated.

All of the Guardian Angel robots had names to match, which was bad enough, but like every other aspect of life, things could always be worse—he could've gotten stuck with an Ieiael. Try saying that when you wake up needing something in the middle of the night.

Still, if the company had spent more time on quality control and less time coming up with clever naming schemes, he wouldn't be in his current predicament.

He'd cut a choice edit about the whole thing—finally hitting the astronomical co-pay, taking delivery, spending ninety blessed days with his Guardian Angel, gaining enough self-confidence to release himself from his shell of self-protection at long last, and then running face-first into day ninety-one.

When Elemiah abruptly stopped working, Tom discovered that the warranty for the heavenly piece of junk conveniently expired on day ninety. To add insult to injury, the government required a deductible more expensive than the original co-pay to be met in order to pay for such costly repairs. There'd been no choice but to return to human home health workers like Myrna, the hitch being that the government wouldn't pay for such care for at least five years after dishing out for the ludicrously expensive paperweight taking up space in the corner.

Tom used to watch the edit all the time, steeping himself in his own misery like one of his perverted clients, but he eventually had to sell the master to Myrna in order to retain her under the table and thus stay in his apartment. In fact, he'd been forced to trade his entire catalog to her over the last handful of years, and all that just for a two-hour visit in the morning and again at night by one of her cronies.

He pressed the back of his skull against his headrest. When he did it just right, he could feel the MD implant above his ear and almost remember what Nessie looked like. He'd traded her away with everything else, reliant now on the incomplete fragments of an organic memory well out of practice for the highlights of his past.

"I'm all done out here," the home health aide said, sliding his bedroom curtain open the rest of the way. It wasn't Myrna. It hadn't been for a long time—not since she'd merged her two main hustles into something threatening legitimacy. Even though this one had been a constant over the last few weeks, Tom couldn't quite remember her name. Emmalyn sounded about right, but so did Emmaline. And Evelyn. Long gone were the days when he'd been compelled to get to know his helpers and entertain them with conversation. Now all he wanted were mute, obedient arms that did what he told them without argument.

"Do you have the edit ready?" she asked.

He'd been working one day in advance for the last few weeks, but he'd run out of interesting ideas even earlier. He'd pissed his sheets last night just so he could record Emmaline cleaning him up this morning. Myrna would take it, but only out of pity.

He glanced at the desktop computer he'd sold and now rented back from his former helper. "In the drive," he said. "Can you plug me in before you go?"

She nodded and did as he asked, then grabbed the data card for her boss. "See you tonight," she said.

"I won't be here," he replied.

She twisted back toward him, her hand on the door handle. "What do you mean?"

"This is my last day in the apartment. They're coming to take me in a few hours."

"What do you mean take you? Take you where?"

"A place where people like me can be forgotten. An institution."

She let go of the handle and took a step toward him, concern creasing her face. She must've been new to the business. "No way. The government—"

"Stop," Tom said. "I've been through it all. I'm done."

"But what about your family? Your parents?"

"Gone." They'd died shortly after Tom had come of age, one after the other, the legacy of a starter apartment built on the dirty remains of a forgotten battery plant. Any inheritance would've cost Tom his government health insurance, so it went to obscure relatives removed once or twice in theory and infinitely more so in practice. He wondered if those estranged relations would reemerge to claim his body when the time came—vintage MD hardware could fetch a pretty penny. He would've sold it off long ago himself if he hadn't grown so attached to it. Literally. Removal meant dementia at the very least, though perhaps that would be preferable where he was headed.

"I'm so sorry," she said.

He shrugged, one of the few gestures he could still

approximate. "Such is life."

"Tell me where this place is. I'll bring you pancit. I make mine with hot dogs."

Tom burped up the sweet whey and watery dust notes of his tube feed. "I'll give the address to Myrna," he said, knowing he wouldn't. That part of his life ended today.

Emmaline seemed to appreciate it nonetheless. "Ingat," she said. "I'll pray for you."

"Palaam," he said, flexing his limited Tagalog.

And then she was gone.

As the sound of Emmalyn shutting the door diminished into silence, Tom found himself diminishing just the same. The food pump whirred, the ventilator blew, the Foley trickled, but none of those sounds were his own. He was like Elemiah now—a broken machine in need of a scrapyard.

He thought about downloading his day so far to the desktop. He'd grabbed whatever pirated rough footage from his life had surfaced on the web on a whim the night before, but hadn't had time to check it yet. Maybe he could cut one last edit to save on his MD and look back upon fondly once at his new home, like he had from every diminishing plateau of his disease progression since he'd first gotten his implant.

Every one of those plateaus had seemed a bedrock trough at the time, but through the gift of retrospect had been exposed as a halcyon summit from the new view far below. Perhaps one day he'd look back upon his time in the institution with the same yearning nostalgia he now felt for his government-sanctioned time with Myrna or his rainy high school run-in with Adam

Adjamian and Nessie.

Or maybe, just maybe, he'd look back from a height now impossible to fathom, rich and privately insured from the edits he had yet to cut, mined from miseries he had yet to endure.

Either way, he'd keep shaving off slices of himself until he ran out of tissue, desperately striving to resonate with the world against longer and longer odds. If he dug deep enough, maybe he'd even be remembered. For a while, at least.

He cleared his throat, keenly aware of his need for a suctioning.

End program.

Bang the Drum
Andy Dibble

When the messenger told me his king was about to be a father, I offered my congratulations. But I did not agree to read the princeling's karma.

The messenger's own karma hung from his shoulders, light and clear. Tracing its weave, I knew he lived a past life in a heaven full of geese and stars. He wore a turban of fine bright linen. His beard was trimmed, his motions practiced.

King Suddhodana had not shamed me by sending a lowly courier. On another day, I would have considered his request. But today, I was on a hunt.

"Asita, you are a reasonable man. A sage. Perhaps we can come to some agreement? The king has a rather *singular* son," said the messenger.

"Not unless you know the whereabouts of a demon named Tamisra." I'd spotted her some weeks ago. Since, I pursued her through the lawless tracks of the forest, the topless Himalaya, and flying the paths of the air. But still she evaded me. I meant to return her to hell.

"There is a woman by that name in the prisons of Kapilavatsu."

"Truly?"

"Yes. The king charges me with knowing all the goings-on of his palace."

"What crime did she commit?"

He looked at me strangely. Must everyone believe the sage Asita divines truth effortlessly, like a swan separates water from mud? "She plowed the fields of four families with salt and castrated the court astrologer."

Crimes of infertility. She must be the Tamisra I sought. "If I could speak with your prisoner, I'd be glad to read the prince's karma."

The messenger agreed at once. Why shouldn't he? Greater kings than Suddhodana paid handsomely for my readings.

I needed to determine how Tamisra had escaped hell. Other demons might exploit her method too. She could be the first of an invasion.

But on the way, the coincidence struck me. Suddhodana's soldiers snared precisely the demon I sought. And just as his messenger had reason to visit me?

How strange. Sometimes karma surprises even me.

•

The prison was dank pens with stolid wooden bars and coarse earth. Prisoners crouched in the vault of gloom near the walls. There was a line of bronze pinchers, forks, and saws against the wall nearest the whipping pole. A grim place, and chilly. But my stay would not be long.

To mundane eyes, Tamisra appeared no more demonic than any other woman. But my eyes saw her karma wound around her, like lianas strangling a tree. It was black and blistered by lifetimes in hell. Demon karma. I saw this as surely as the mundane eye ogles charred flesh.

"How did you escape hell?" I said through the bars.

Tamisra emerged from the back of her cell, haughty as black Kali crushing a god underfoot. "When I was born."

How could one with such ruined karma throw off her demon lives and achieve rebirth as a human? I squinted to better reckon her karma. By the layered mess of scar tissue, Tamisra suffered long in hell, one hundred lifetimes at least. If after such a mangled garland of lives, she finally clinched a precious human birth, her present crimes would doubtlessly plunge her in hell again. I could almost pity her.

But I knew she was lying. "No, I think you escaped with the new moon." In which case she possessed some poor woman—or the corpse of one. That's why I spied just one karmic accretion, not two. Without a host, nothing bound her to the middle realms of men. The sun and moon would conspire with her foul karma. She would still be in hell.

"You asked. And I told you the truth."

"I do not believe one trapped in hell so long could be reborn as a human."

She chuckled. "I see my karma better than you, great sage. For karma is subtle in its recompenses. Karma revealed itself to me, so I'd know the eons I suffered, rebirth after rebirth. So that I would see and despair." She smiled wanly. "Do you know what hell was like for me?"

"I have seen hell in others' karma."

"An image of a thing is not the thing, Asita. And you did

not answer my question."

"Tell me of your hell, then."

"In a past world-cycle, I was born in a colossal pot of boiling oil, so huge one plunges downward for a thousand years and tumbles upward a thousand more, buffeted by convection." She shivered, a torch flame tugged by wind. "The oil was just half my hell. The other half was anger, impotent rage against every sentient being imagined or real, anyone that roused hate in me and thereby fouled my karma. I imagined effigies of them, all of them, swirling in the oil, their insides flayed as mine were, invading every orifice, killing me, birthing me again, reforming me like wax."

How gullible does she think I am? A boiling oil hell? There could never be a pot so huge. To think cookery could be a fixture of the universe! But she is contained and marked for execution. What is the harm in letting her prattle on?

"But there was one mercy. Once every two thousand years, for a single breath, my head broke the surface. I could cry out a word—a name, a plea—before plunging down again into the heaving vat. So I did what I could. I cried for help, screaming the name 'Dipankara' with my one breath and two thousand years later crying out 'Kashyapa' and two thousand years later 'Vipashyin': divine names, names of omniscient buddhas. One of them would take pity on me eventually."

"A buddha pitied you? You?"

She ignored my jibe. "And so I was swept around, coveting a name as I rose higher and higher to the zenith of my hell. I sucked air and managed, 'Avalok—', but the undertow pulled me under. A wasted chance! Two thousand years to botch a name! I managed only three rushed syllables that could not be the name of anyone. But through the agony, I considered the no-one I invoked. How wonderful it must be to be Avalok, he who was never born and could never suffer what I have suffered."

"You must have envied him."

"No!" She struck the bars hard with negation. "It was compassion that saved me. I considered how liberating it would be for me, for all my compatriots in all the hells, if we were never born, for all beings in all the worlds to never be born. *That* is how I escaped ten-thousand births in hell."

This act was quite overdone. "You've had your fun. No moment of fellow-feeling, of compassion, could free you from an absurd hell."

She smiled like a guest tolerating the child of her host.

"Next you will tell me that you castrated the king's astrologer because of the love you bear for the children he will never conceive."

Tamisra's smile was the last sliver of an eclipsing moon. "If I speak truth, may you see the buddha of this age but not live to hear his teaching."

•

She had tried to curse me, or aped at cursing. That must be the end of all civil discussion. I turned on my heel and left.

Next to see the king. There was a young man with tight white lips and dark eyes on his way down the sunlit stairs leading from the prison. He gripped a many-tailed whip. His karma flailed like a burning viper.

But the lambent glow of his prior lives tickled me. I traced the karmic fibers and marveled at the change. Eighteen lives ago he was a king of kings, turning the wheel of empire over all the lands of men. Everything the noonday sun touched was his domain. In the life before, he reposed twenty-thousand years in the Tushita heaven. Once, long ago, he ruled a herd of four-thousand elephants, trumpeting in the foothills of the Vindhya mountains, confounding poachers who sought his opal tusks. At the limit of my sight, I puzzled out a brief life in which he was a selfless hare, who roasted his own flesh to feed a starving child. The blisters of hell nowhere marked his karma.

"Let me pass," he growled, yanking my attention to the present. And whirling back, I saw the livid gash in his karma, where rage kindled. It was not long ago, no more than a moon.

The weave of his dhoti was fine. A sacred thread crossed his bare chest. Tattooed star charts wound over his arms. I thought him Viplava, king Suddhodana's court astrologer. Meaning he was the man Tamisra had castrated.

"My errand is urgent," he said, not so hot as before. No doubt, his errand was whatever sorry business that whip was for.

"Viplava?" I said.

"And you?"

"Asita."

Tamisra said I would see the Buddha. Him? Perhaps she preys on those that tread the path toward buddha-hood? She just guessed he and I would meet, and I would see the seed of final enlightenment in him and know that she plucked it out by souring him with rage.

"It shames me not to have recognized you," said Viplava. He pressed his palms together and bowed.

I greeted him likewise. "And it shames me not to have met you sooner." Until now, I associated his name with the wry joke: Doomseer Viplava is so keen to spell disaster, he predicted nine of the last three demon invasions. But seeing his karma—pure save the recent enmity—I knew that joke was vicious gossip.

I would pry, but carefully. "Your errand—it requires a whip?"

"Ah." He let the whip dangle behind him. "King Suddhodana sentenced a prisoner to five lashings every day until her execution." His many-tailed whip glint with iron barbs, to make every lashing count.

Viplava continued, "But the king has a son today." His karma hissed and burst into envious conflagration. Such a shame to see brute fury gorge upon his sterling pedigree of lives. "The king's joy does not permit him to order his jailers to punish anyone. So the duty falls on me."

"We are brahmin," I said simply. "The rod of punishment is not our burden."

"A demon-hunting sage questions whether a brahmin may do the duty of a warrior?"

"I hunt demons to uplift the kingdoms of men, to end mayhem."

"And I do justice." He was sincere. And, I thought, a little mad. "We are more alike than you think, Asita."

"Forgive me. I was only surprised. Come, Viplava, let us go congratulate the king on this happy day. A son and an heir!"

But Viplava would not be distracted. "You go ahead. I will join you in the assembly hall when I'm through."

"If you mean to meet Tamisra, she is wily, powerful. We'd best go together."

He paused only a moment before relenting, "Then come. You've seen sights more gruesome in some life."

But why, I wondered, must I see them again?

•

Tamisra was bound to a post at the center of the prison. The wood beneath her wrists was smooth from the hand oils of many penitents.

The guard Chandaka stood as equanimitously as the whipping pole. Tamisra eyed him warily. Chandaka's hands were callused and speckled with burn marks. The calluses had broken here and there into blisters.

I could guess why. He held the knotted whips, the hot tongs, the scalding oils. Any other day, he would be Tamisra's punisher.

His karma bore the calluses but no blisters. Torture was his duty, and he did his duty with detachment, so his karma grew tough and woody. To him, suffering is essential to life, to all lives, like saltiness to salt.

Tamisra paid Viplava no mind, though he loomed at her back like the god of death. To her, Viplava's wrath was just nature, as certain as a thing foretold. She castrated him, so he seeks revenge. Malice begets punishment. Karma produces its like.

But she acknowledged me. "If you're with him, your grasp of karma is even poorer than I thought, Asita."

"Don't mind her," said Viplava.

Tamisra went on, not speaking to anyone in particular. "In another life of mine, long ago, there was another that tried to whip me. Passion seized him but he froze before bringing the lash down, stayed without twitching. He breathed several long breaths before I found the courage to ask why."

Viplava snarled and in one motion furrowed bloody lines in her back.

Tamisra bit back a scream. "Don't you want to know what he said?"

"No talk." Viplava's whip-arm reared like a cobra.

"What did he say?" I said.

Tamisra chuckled. "'I'm punishing an angry man.'"

Viplava cracked the whip with a snarl. Tamisra's back arched like a cat's. She bit back her scream again.

Another lash, one she couldn't anticipate. Tamisra shrieked and pain silhouetted her karma but, like green wood, nothing kindled. Resentment didn't singe her karma. But it rode this peerless man, Viplava?

But what in karma is just? Karma is fortune's wheel. We ride it up and down again, and maybe never up again.

Another lash, another scream, another and another. That exceeded the five king Suddhodana prescribed.

"Think of your karma, Viplava!" I said.

He whirled on me, brandishing the whip. He was a different man, more demon than man. "This is *justice*."

Only my knowledge of his better self lent me the courage to speak. "If not for your sake, then for the king's. Do not stain the day he became a father with ugliness."

"Salt her wounds." Viplava shoved the whip in Chandaka's hand. "I'll return tomorrow."

•

As Viplava and I approached the king's assembly hall, I took small solace knowing the astrologer bathed. Rage doesn't wash off. He didn't show it, but what fool seethes in front of his king? Looking deeper, I plumbed heat, like Tamisra's hell, swirling oil, imagined effigies, paroxysms of rage, rage begetting rage. I must confront him, as one man to another, or his resentment would surely drive him to hell in his next life or one not far off.

But now it was impossible. The assembly hall of the king stretched before us. Brocade drapes studded with beryl and moonstone hung between pillars of tawny sandalwood. Tapestries of demon armies washing futilely against brilliant formations of chariots overlaid the lacquered walls on either side. Smoke from the sacrificial fire wafted in so the newborn prince would breathe it and live one-hundred autumns. In the center of the court was the king's throne cast in the likenesses of the horse-headed Ashvins, the twin sons of the sun.

Ministers and attendant sages chattered about the newborn prince like monkeys in a banyan tree. One faction of sages prognosticated that he would be an emperor, conquer all the kingdoms of the world, and rule them justly. A second faction assured king Suddhodana that the prince would renounce worldly life, attain enlightenment as a buddha, teach others, and liberate multitudes from birth and death.

"Viplava and Asita have come," said the king. "They must see prince Siddhartha."

The chattering cut-off. The sages and ministers drew back, revealing the king on his throne.

In his lap was the softly sleeping prince. Siddhartha glowed golden as the cosmic mountain Meru. Delicate webbing spanned his fingers. The soles of his darling feet were arched like a heavenly dancer's and emblazoned with wheel-emblems. The curl on his brow glowed like a star plucked from the bosom of the night. His eyes were agate-blue and limpid as a gazelle's. In expression, he was as austere as Tamisra when she vowed I would one day see the Buddha.

Viplava cooed. "He is magnificent, lord, as glorious as Indra enthroned in heaven. It is certain that he will be either a world-ruling monarch or the buddha of this age and liberate the whole world from rebirth and death."

"But you cannot say which?" said the king.

"I cannot say," said Viplava. That was expertly done. Neither faction had reason to bicker if "doom-seer" Viplava pronounced great tidings. Because Viplava offered an intermediate position, both factions could save face.

Suddhodana nodded graciously toward Viplava. But he said, "Asita, you are renowned, even amongst this esteemed company. If there is some omen others have missed, some black stroke of karma that will stain my son's days, tell me. It is better that a father know, than that he lives in fear."

I pressed my palms together and bowed to the king. "Lord, may I hold him?"

The king gave consent. I approached, held the child, beheld him. As I surveyed the miracle of his karma, hot tears stained my cheeks.

The king gasped, eyes wide and trembling.

"The prince's karma is pure," I hastened to explain, "unsullied for as far as my third eye can see. I weep only for my own fate." The child's karma was airy and clear as Kashi muslin. I reached for it, but it slipped through my fingers like a breeze.

This child would renounce his royal inheritance, take up the ascetic life, and at last attain final enlightenment. He would become the Buddha and ferry multitudes across the ocean of existence to nirvana.

But as his karma ripened and flourished, mine reassembled. I would not live long enough to hear his teaching. I thought my karma pure, but it bedeviled me just as I was nearing the end.

"Sadhu! Sadhu!" said the king. "Chandaka, take up the drum. March through my prisons, cry amnesty."

Viplava recoiled, sputtered a moment. "Don't you want to know what they did?"

"I have a son, Viplava. The most excellent son a man could have. This day is beyond Justice."

"But lord, the executioner will starve if not given his man." There stood Viplava, at the front of the ministers, his karma flung over the court, a conqueror's banner. Surely, he pictured criminals rioting from the prisons, repeating their wrongs, sowing chaos. The safety of the kingdom demanded their containment.

"One sowed four fields with salt," Viplava said. "She would render every field in the kingdom barren, given the chance."

How wrong I was. Justice was just Viplava's excuse. Blinded by the wrong done to him, he pressed all criminals into an indiscriminate lump—all bent-over, hell-bound, depraved, loathing the sun and moon and everyone that stands upright beneath them.

Knots of ministers chattered about the dangers of the king's proposal: fear of assault in the city, reduction in tax levies. How many craftsmen will be afraid to leave their homes? Would the army be reduced to almshouse attendants? What of the impact on trade?

But their karma roiled, became turbid, became green, hissing self-servingly about loss of luxury, who the king would blame if the kingdom spiraled out of joint. If they continued as they were, they would live future lives as hungering ghosts with ponderous bellies and necks thin as needles, unable to swallow. Their greed would fester and they would suffer rebirth again, propagating their karma, more lives as ghosts, more greed, greed begetting greed.

Like a lion among his cubs, the king bore the squabbling, and joy did not flee his face. At last, he raised his hand to signal calm. "Asita, you have been silent, and alongside your silence, every other voice reaches my ear like haggling in the marketplace."

Today king Suddhodana dwelt beyond punishment and blame, but his karma embraced his son's, entwined among the court, and then rambled out among the squares and boulevards of Kapilavatsu. I knew the meaning: he loved his son more than all his subjects together. Such unequal care would eventually find him out. If not in this life, then another by the rigid law of karma.

The god of death gripped the world, and all wandered like

puppets on karmic strings. "There must be an end to it," I murmured.

"What's that?" said the king.

The strings of karma were not unseverable. I could see it. "Lord, may the salt-sower Viplava speaks of be brought to us?"

"Lord—"

The king raised a hand, silenced Viplava, sharply enough to cut the first string.

•

When Chandaka led Tamisra into the throne room at spear point, she wore a fresh shawl and tunic, but the wounds on her back still stunk of blood and salt. Her presence was so far outside the norm, no one found words for their dismay.

Except Viplava. "Lord, Asita violates all custom, shames you on this happy day by bringing this degenerate woman among us."

"The world is yoked by karma because it continues as it has," I said. "We must make a change. Viplava, what do you feel for this woman?"

Viplava struggled to bar the storm from his face.

"Answer Asita's question," said the king.

"I hate her. Like I hate the day of my death."

"Tamisra, what do you feel for this man?" I said.

"For him, nothing," she said. "But I'm glad he will curse no being with birth and death."

"Look, Viplava," I said, "She means you no harm—"

"Means me no harm! Consider what she's taken from me. I see the little prince and..."

"Go ahead," said the king.

"I *envy*. I will never have a son so excellent." Tears glistened in his eyes as he choked off a sob. He issued a ragged breath. "I will never have a son at all."

Tamisra cut a childless man, but rehashing her crime wouldn't help Viplava. "Viplava, any man can envy the king for fathering a boy so excellent, but the great man envies nothing," I said.

Viplava stammered with incredulity. "Asita, you wrong me. Do not forget who the victim is here." So Viplava still recognized only victims, evil-doers, and an uneven equation between them.

"See her, bleeding, wretched. *You* did that. And for what? Every wrong she's done you, karma has done to you innumerable times before. Doubtlessly, you've lived eunuch lives, childless lives. We all have."

He grumbled, his retort dissipating.

I offered Viplava the sleepy infant. "The little prince can punish no one. Not today, not ever. Be like him."

Viplava's tears fell on the prince's cheeks. "I was wrong earlier, when I said I didn't know. The prince will be a buddha."

I turned to Tamisra. "How can you feel nothing for this man?"

"He's only karma, mindless, driving the world, proliferating itself."

I shook my head. "Detachment is not enough. Nor is compassion only for the unborn. Identify with the man before you."

She regarded Viplava, not with scorn or resentment, but like one prisoner regards another marched away for execution. Rebirth after rebirth, karma was the executioner. It was an impotent look, but it could make all the difference.

"With your leave, lord, I would have Tamisra hold your son."

Suddhodana frowned. "Isn't she a demon?"

"She was a demon. Now she is a woman. She's committed grave wrongs, but so have we all, in this life or another."

Suddhodana blinked. He nodded stiffly.

Viplava did not protest. He sidled toward Tamisra. Her hand brushed his hand when she accepted the shining prince. Viplava did not startle at her touch.

Tamisra brushed one of Viplava's tears from the prince's cheek. She brushed another. Her tears replaced his, rain from a clear sky.

"Why do you weep?" I said.

"I wanted an end to birth and death, would've torn the seed out of every man to do it. But if I had, this darling child would not be born." She twirled her finger around the curl on the prince's forehead.

"Then dry your tears," I said. "The birth and death of multitudes will end with him. Yes, we must wait a little longer, some of us must wait, but it need not be with idleness or selfish anticipation. Let us do as the king commanded. Open the prisons, bang the drum of amnesty because one day the little prince will bang the drum of the deathless."

The Vulture Man
Kai Calo

Death liked to take up residence in the most ordinary places. Hector Velasquez stared out the window as he and his aunt were stopped at a red light. A dead cat lay on the roadside.

"It's sad, I know," said his aunt. She tightened her grip on the steering wheel. There was doubt in her voice regarding whether she could explain the realities of cats being struck by cars to a twelve-year-old whose sister had succumbed to the same fate. She cleared her throat. "Animal control will come, *mijo*. It's… a part of life."

Hector could not speak.

There was a man he had not seen. A man near the cat.

A man with vultures.

He wore a black trench coat and black pants, so black the sunlight was consumed by its intensity. He was tall, sallow, and sickly. His eyes peered from cave-like holes. He stood over the roadkill, the vultures scampering around him and the carcass. One perched on his slanted shoulder and the rest paused, simultaneously raising their wings as if in salute. Another moment and they began to eat the cat.

Hector turned his head and stared out the front window.

"There's a vulture problem in Florida," his aunt said.

Hector was still.

"Hector?"

"T-The man," Hector said once he could breathe.

"What man?"

Hector stared straight ahead. The man frightened him, but he swallowed the lump in his throat and made himself turn to seek the dark figure.

"The man who…"

He was gone.

Hector pushed the back of his head into his seat. He blinked while his fists clenched at his shorts.

"Never mind," he said.

The light turned green and the car accelerated.

•

Everything changed after the tragedy. Hector's father could not cope with his loss, so he'd gone to a place that would protect him from himself. Hector's mother had left when he was young. With nowhere to go, he went to his aunt Abigail's house in Florida. She'd said it was the least she could do after hearing about Valentina.

Now he sat glancing out the window of his new school, his chin propped in his palm. His teacher's voice was a distant drone. He tapped his pencil on a piece of paper, flipping it along his knuckles, and then yawned.

It was raining. There was a group of vultures hunched like gargoyles around a raccoon. Hector observed their ritualistic waddling amid the dead, spotting the glisten of urine as it slid down their legs. The rain let up and he witnessed them spreading their wings. For a moment it was like they were mystical argosies in a perpetual state of departure (or arrival, depending on one's view). The summer sun reflected off the hard keratin of their plumage in white shards, contrasting the night of their cloaked bodies.

"They're sunbathing," said a voice at his side.

Hector jumped in his seat, his chest tightening as he looked to see a familiar face. Mrs. Raymond had brown hair and dark eyes. They showed kindness for him. He liked her but felt uneasy.

"It's called the *horaltic* pose," she added, pointing to the birds drawn on his paper. She looked out the window and crossed her arms. "They do that so they can dry off and warm up."

He didn't reply.

"Are you interested in animals, Hector?"

He shook his head. She reached for Hector's desk and pulled his drawing from under his forearms. He was supposed to have been reading with the class.

"You like drawing?" she asked.

Hector shook his head again.

She studied his drawing. Hector noticed the other kids staring. They whispered. He felt like a stranger.

Mrs. Raymond gave him back his paper and walked away. Several of his classmates snickered. Mrs. Raymond came back from her desk and held out a packet for Hector to take. Inside was a lead pencil and a charcoal stick.

"It sure looks like you like to draw," she said.

Hector pulled out a piece of charcoal and held it in his hand. It left a residue of shadow powder on the pads of his fingers.

He put it to the paper, hypnotized, but Mrs. Raymond spoke.

"You should start signing your work, Mr. Velasquez," she said. She went and wrote a question pertaining to their reading on the board, adding, "*After* class."

Hector put the charcoal down and sighed. He looked out the window, expecting to see the vultures feasting.

But he saw *him*.

Those piercing eyes.

Hector froze. Why was *he* there? Why was the Vulture Man following him?

At that moment, it didn't matter what Mrs. Raymond said. Hector took the charcoal and began to draw. He couldn't bring himself to look at the Vulture Man, but he'd seen him twice now. Enough to start a rough sketch. He emptied his worries and fears onto that paper, and despite the hollow skeleton watching him, he felt better in a way he couldn't describe.

He was so enthralled he did not hear the bell.

•

Sun penetrated the kitchen shades. Saturday morning, cartoons, wrapped in blankets while fall made the leaves change. Their father reading in his armchair. Valentina with blocks on the floor. She looked up and spoke in a small voice.

"Look," and her finger pointed outside.

He blinked. They were outside now. The sun made him squint. The road was tar black. She ran and laughed. He cried when he learned of fragility. Both discovered the banal deadliness of a car in motion.

Then he was in his house, but it was different. There was

darkness creeping from the opposite side of the room. A shadowy figure was in the corner. Reality changed. Decay seeped. Wallpaper shriveled and curled. The carpet grew black and mildewed, emitting a musty odor. Valentina's colorful toys, her plush rainbow unicorn, dulled and patinaed. The wave of decay obscured the room. Vultures surrounded them, waddling next to Valentina. One lurched closer. It curved its head and pecked at her rosy cheek. A strip of flesh came back, hanging from the creature's sharp beak. Hector gasped.

He woke sweating. Where was he?

He was not home.

•

Whether caused by adolescence or grief, Hector decided the Vulture Man was a monster created by his imagination, and nothing more. And monsters weren't real. In fact, they were nothing compared to death, grief, change, and sadness. *Those* were real. Still, he drew the Vulture Man a lot. The sketches cluttered his room. They piled on his aunt's coffee table. But they didn't look right.

He gnawed at his fingernail while sitting on the couch, squinting at his work. Something was missing. He took out some pens and attempted to fix the details. The face was too blank, too vacant. There was more to the man than that strange expression and horrible, vacuous stare. It was hard to capture in a portrait, and Hector wasn't that skilled.

He looked around. The décor of the one-story home was cozy but eclectic, with folk art from different cultures decorating the walls. Clay figurines stood atop the back panel of the stove. In

Hector's room, there was a print of a black and white skeleton woman with a large hat. On the couch were bright pillows shaped like *calaveras*.

Hector punched one of the pillows in frustration and went back to his drawing. There was an urgency to get it right. At least the *feel*. There was an absolute terror about the Vulture Man. Hector felt it in his stomach, a premonitory tummy-ache, like the lingering moment before a stranger reached for your shoulder. That was the scariest thing about the Vulture Man—there was no *knowing* where he was. More an *awareness* that he could be anywhere, like the vultures atop the utility poles near their house. Were they his vultures? Hector avoided them anyway.

He groaned and flipped his drawing, beginning again with da Vincian dedication on the other side, sketching loosely until an hour had passed. His back felt sore from leaning over the coffee table, so he stood and stretched, ambling towards the window to see the Volusia tree with the tire swing in the front yard. He yawned, rubbed his eyes, then halted.

It was *him*.

The Vulture Man perched like one of his vultures on the swing. His eyes were wide, white orbs of Murano glass stuck in darkened sockets. His stare was penetrating. As the swing moved in the breeze, his head stayed motionless. He did not blink.

Hector was still. He wanted to back away, run, but he couldn't move.

The Vulture Man was like a living statue swathed in sable, the visible skin of his hands, neck and face a sharp contrast of chalky, sodium carbonate and marble. Then, he leaned forward off the swing; it didn't shift with his movement but kept its gentle swaying as if there'd been no additional force but the breeze. His vultures watched and spread their wings. The Man walked towards the window.

Hector's breath was imprisoned in his lungs. All that came out was a strangled croaking sound from the back of his throat, as if his voice box had suddenly dropped into his stomach and been doused with bile. He was a mouse glued to a trap.

The Vulture Man neared the window, stopped at the glass, and looked in. Hector had the briefest thought that now he could draw the face better. He could portray the dark, haggard trench coat with its tattered elbows and the dark pants and shirt. He could depict the vertical drop in the man's shape, his height and narrow width, and the nasal cavity in the center of his face that was a hollowed, beak-like hole.

He's turning towards the doorstep. He's going for the handle!

Hector darted for the door and turned the bolt.

"Go away," he whispered.

The handle didn't turn. It didn't even budge. There was no noise, no sign the Vulture Man attempted to breach the entryway. Hector breathed in relief.

Then the door vibrated. It wavered, and the wood lost its mass and density, lost its physical properties. It became nothing but the visual residue of a door. A black figure stepped through the wood as if it were a portal. Hector shrieked. The Vulture Man's stare was a car coming straight for him, like oncoming headlights. He was transfixed with terror, bolted to the ground like an inanimate object. The Vulture Man stepped closer. Hector felt the earth spin. His vision blurred.

"Hector?"

Hector heard his name and recognized his aunt enter the garage door with bags of groceries in her arms. She dropped the bags and raced over to him.

"Hector, what's wrong?" she asked, panicked.

She looked down. Hector followed her line of sight. He'd wet himself. He felt the urine slide down his leg to the floor where it puddled at his feet, soaking his white socks yellow. His aunt rubbed his shoulders and felt his forehead.

"You're so pale, *mijo*," she said and hugged him.

No discussion was had about what happened. At least, not with him. Hector could hear his aunt on the phone in her bedroom late into the evening when she thought he was asleep. She was worried about his state of mind. He'd been distant and was failing school. All he was doing was drawing. Was it okay to let him draw? Was that how he was dealing? She thought maybe he saw things, that he was having daymares. Repressing the death of his sister. Could she take care of him? Would she have to place him somewhere else?

But it would not get rid of the Vulture Man. He was everywhere and nowhere; he was a fact of life, unable to be stopped.

Hector could not avoid him.

He had no choice.

In his room, Hector got his charcoal, his pencils, and his drawing pad. He forced himself to look out the window at the pale face hovering like a disembodied skull in the night. The gentle scratch of his pencil calmed him. It would all be finished soon.

•

Hector avoided the creaky floorboard in the hall, the one his aunt stepped on thirty minutes prior. He knew she was in bed and sleeping. He crept into the living room and silently left through the front door.

Night was still. The air was warm. The moon held a lonesome beauty.

Hector walked through a dark parking lot. From the outside, he appeared a diligent young man, but inside he was trembling. He followed the signs: a decayed armadillo picked clean, a fat snake, a skunk. The carcasses eyes—if they hadn't already been eaten—were hollow, with a tremendous vacancy that made him shiver. When he came across some foxes, a big one and two small ones, he became queasy. But it was the right direction.

Then, when he found what he'd been searching for, he felt his throat tighten. They were like Skeksis, hunched and clawing, picking apart the fresh carrion, digging into the protruding entrails and the rotting anus of some unrecognizable creature. Hector gulped. A tall, cloaked figure was with the vultures.

"H-hey," he said. "*You.*"

The man turned. His face became visible over the sharp angle of his shoulder. Hector fought the urge to run, holding firm as that vacant gaze caught him in its sight. He threw a piece of paper. It landed in the space between him and the Vulture Man, unrolling to reveal the image of a ghost white man cloaked in a long black coat, ebony birds framing his austere countenance. His nose was black, a naked skull's open nose cavity, like a painted beak in the center of his face. His eyes were obsidian, gleaming.

Hector scrambled to take off his backpack and retrieved a large pad of drawing paper, a charcoal stick, and a pencil with an eraser. He knelt and drew. The Vulture Man suddenly snapped into movement; he marched towards the portrait and stared at the image. His steps were mechanical and quick.

Despite the fear, Hector continued to draw, studying the man in his entirety, and after a few moments he felt calm. He smiled.

"See?" he asked the Vulture Man, tilting his drawing pad. "It looks like you. I've seen the birds; I watch them. I see you, and I know what you look like. I'm not afraid of you anymore."

There was a long pause, as if Hector's words had to travel lightyears to the man's decayed ear holes. So far were they from one another; Hector, full of life and heat; the Vulture Man, dead and cold. The Vulture Man opened his mouth. Hector thought he would speak, but instead the man vomited a semi-digested lump of meat. It fell onto the completed drawing on the ground. The act itself was not scary, but the smell made Hector feel sick. It was rancid, rotting flesh, with nature's bilious stomach acid designed to digest flesh. It dribbled down the Vulture Man's chin and Hector almost vomited too.

The smell became unbearable. But it wasn't the awful reek that made Hector bolt upright, nor was it the gurgling shriek he heard. It was her.

His sister.

She came from the shadows, glowing like a fading star. Hector's eyes became wet. She looked like she did before she died, but he knew. It lingered in the back of his mind, and despite how unbearable it was, he knew. He knew… she was gone. And he could join her. Or he could fight back.

Without taking his eyes off his subject, he sank to the ground and picked up his drawing pad and charcoal. He started to sketch another drawing of the Vulture Man. As he did, the distant star that was Valentina closed in, looking on his drawing. Hector didn't stop, even when he felt her presence. Her small body dimmed the streetlamps and, when Hector's eyes darted involuntarily up, he saw the limned outline that surrounded her, but his focus was not her; the Vulture Man was his subject.

Hector kept sketching until the image was clear, then ripped the page from the pad and tossed it to the ground. He didn't wait to start another. The sounds of vomiting could be heard, and the smell was again filling his nostrils. Still, he remained, holding back a gag until a small piece of vomit landed on his sketch. Grabbing at his mouth, he looked up. Valentina's chin was wet with bile. Her eyes were hollow. Hector grit his teeth and forced himself to finish the sketch, then ripped the ruined drawing, tossing it atop the other. He began again.

But a shrill shriek emitted into the night made him flinch. The Vulture Man was approaching, his movements now plodding and slow, urging anxiety. The shrieking became louder, and Hector made the mistake of letting his charcoal fall as he peered into vacuous eyes. Valentina vomited for the final time. A partially digested piece of meat in the shape of a torn plush horse—no, a once vibrant unicorn, landed square atop Hector's drawing pad. He shot up.

"Go away!" he screamed at the Vulture Man. "Stop haunting me!"

Another protesting shriek.

"I won't stop!" Hector threw the drawing pad in its entirety at the Vulture Man and took a small blank booklet from his pocket, glaring to see the Vulture Man in full view. "I won't roll over and die! I'll never stop!"

Another horrible shriek. It was so loud, and the smell of rotting flesh so powerful, that Hector could hardly stand it. But he would not stop drawing; he would not let the Vulture Man win. He had to draw. It made him alive.

There was another shriek, but it did not faze him. He expected it, but it didn't come from the Vulture Man. It came from the nearby street. He turned to the source of the sound and saw her. His sister. She was running.

He started running too. He sprinted as fast as he could, following her into that open space of road. The lines reflected beneath his gait, and suddenly a light was rapidly coming. He whirled around straight into headlights.

A screech and a thud and another screech and a horrible, rasping trill.

A man got out of the stopped car.

"Damn bird!" he yelled. He came around to inspect the damage to his bumper and saw the vulture lying on the pavement, lifeless. Then he saw Hector. "What the hell are you doing out here, kid? If that buzzard hadn't flown into my windshield you would have been hit. You wanna' die, kid? Is that what you want? You want to *die*?"

The headlights were dazzling in Hector's eyes, so much that he could only hear the tall man. The rest of him was a dark figure made darker by the shadows.

"No," was all Hector could say. He darted out of the street and didn't stop running until he got home.

When he was at the front door, his aunt woke and scolded him. To her shock, Hector broke down in her arms. She hugged him close and told him it would be alright. He believed her, but not because he wanted to, because he finally knew it was true.

Hector did not see the Vulture Man again, at least, not as the Vulture Man he knew. He would see something abstract, a feeling. He would sense the man in the passage of time, would see him in the wilting of flowers and autumn leaves. In these times, when Hector felt at his weakest, he would not retreat, but would retrieve his drawing pad and sketch whatever beauty he could find. In years to come, he would turn to paints and canvas.

The Vulture Man was gone.

•

The car's hum was a soft droning through the night. The headlights flooded the ground. A large bird was taken into long arms sleeved in black. The other vultures surrounded the car. They were the death eaters, but they did not consume their own. Instead, their comrade was placed on the passenger seat of the vehicle. The door shut and the car began down the road, its destination unknown, always unknown, until it unexpectedly arrived.

The Air Show
Rudy Kremberg

If you wanted the best view of the air show, the beach along Hanlan's Point was the place to be. I'm sure it still is, though I've avoided the area ever since the five of us went there that Labour Day afternoon. No force on earth could drag me back.

We all lived in the same melting pot of a neighbourhood and attended the same school, and while my parents were barely on speaking terms with some of the other parents—you can blame the war—that hadn't stopped us from hanging out together and forming our little gang of airplane fanatics. Of course, our fathers and uncles were our inspiration: Jamie's old man had been a Spitfire ace, Lech's had navigated a Lancaster, Ralph's had lost a leg at Dieppe but his American uncle had scored kills in a Mustang, and Ken's folks had flown Zeros. Ken's uncle had been a kamikaze.

The others liked to tease Ken because he was Japanese, one of the enemy. But I got it even worse.

My dad fought on the German side. He shot down more planes than any of the other dads or uncles—he actually got a medal, but after the war he threw it away. He couldn't or wouldn't tell me his exact tally, just that it was upwards of fifty and he flew a Messerschmitt Bf 109 fighter for the Luftwaffe.

Yeah, I was the really bad guy.

It puzzled me that my dad didn't like to talk about his exploits. Whenever I raised the subject a wary, haunted look would creep into his eyes. Instead of answering my questions he'd lecture me about spending too much time reading *Air War Stories* and building models. When I mentioned I wanted to see the air show with the gang, that we hoped there'd be vintage planes from the war, he went on in German about "insulting the dead" and "messing with cosmic forces"—my translation. He drank too much sometimes, and that was one of those times.

I'd always suspected his drinking was connected with the war, but I didn't know what was behind that spooked-out look. Not until the air show.

•

It started at one that year. Lech's father and older brother dropped us off at the ferry terminal on their way to Exhibition Stadium, where the Argos were playing, and by twelve thirty we were on the part of Toronto Island known as Hanlan's Point, following the chain-link fence that bordered Toronto Island Airport. The beach was on the opposite side of the small airfield, and Jamie's parents were supposed to meet us there after a morning at the art gallery. If I was lucky his sister would be coming with them—I had a secret crush on her.

There wasn't a cloud in the sky as we passed the airport, keeping our eyes peeled for warbirds that might be taking part in the show. An Austin Airways DC-3 and a couple of Cessnas were parked on the tarmac, that was all, and beyond the main runway a few men were standing around, talking. Pilots or ground crew, I assumed.

By a quarter to one we'd reached a bend in the fence. We were setting out along the dirt path that led to the beach through a stretch of trees and dense bushes when a voice spoke up, startling us:

"Hey, kids, you here for the air show?"

Stepping out from behind a thicket was a tall, thin guy in a flight suit, complete with Mae West life jacket, parachute harness and flak helmet, a pair of goggles dangling from his hand. I figured he was one of the pilots we'd passed five minutes ago, though with his delicate pale complexion he looked quite young. He was eyeing me as if he recognized me.

At first I could only nod. I remember noticing a dark stain on his flight suit, over his chest, but didn't make anything of it at the time. For all I knew, he'd come here for no other reason than to take a pee in the bushes, and our encounter was purely a coincidence.

"What's your plane?" I asked him.

"B-24 Liberator." He turned so that I could see the United States Army Air Forces insignia on his shoulder sleeve. "We flew one in '44. It'll be in the show."

"A Liberator," I repeated, thinking of the Airfix model I'd just finished painting. It had to be the most impressive bomber in my collection. "Cool."

The man's eyes narrowed. He seemed to be looking right into me, judging me.

"When I was your age I went to air shows, too," he said. "I thought there was nothing cooler in this world than those planes, just like you guys do. That's why I want to tell you a little secret. Want to hear it?"

Now there was a hint of condescension in his voice, almost contempt. He sounded as young as he looked—too young to have been in the war. That could be misleading, I told myself. I nodded again.

"Look over there." The man gestured towards a gap in the bushes, where another path branched out. The path we were on was nine or ten feet wide, and it twisted and turned for roughly a hundred yards. The secondary path was narrower but a good twenty yards shorter, staying parallel to the airport fence and then curving away slightly. A patch of sand was visible at the other end.

"It's a new path," the man elaborated. "Follow it and you'll have the best view of the show, guaranteed."

"We already know where that is," Ralph said. "The beach."

"Right. But this new path'll take you to a part you couldn't get to before. Nobody could, except…people like us."

"You mean, pilots?"

"Uh-huh. Pilots, too."

I was about to ask if the place he had in mind was a restricted area of the beach that belonged to the airport, but he'd already started down the path.

"Believe me," he said without pausing, "the view's fantastic."

He gave us a wave, then vanished into the bushes. I heard voices by the fence and gathered there was an opening in it, that he'd joined his fellow pilots on the other side.

"What're we waiting for?" Jamie said.

"I don't know if we should trust him," Ralph said. "Where's

his B-24? I didn't see it on the tarmac."

"It must be in a hangar," Jamie said. "C'mon, aren't you guys curious? We can meet up with my parents later."

We all looked down the path again. Were my eyes playing tricks on me, or was there a bit of ground mist building up? It was now ten to one, according to my Timex.

"We should get moving," I said, and led the way.

•

We couldn't have spent more than thirty seconds on the path, half walking and half running. If there was an opening in the airport fence, it was concealed by the bushes. I ran mainly because I was nervous, and I don't think I was the only one. The path itself had something to do with this—the faster we moved, the longer it seemed to get. I had the dreamlike impression we were gaining ground and then falling back a little, gaining and falling back, over and over, and that as we drew closer to the other end we were somehow doing both simultaneously. Adding to the confusion was the mist. Yes, it was definitely there, along the bottom and sides of the path. Plus I couldn't rid myself of the feeling we were being followed. Did I hear a whisper, or was it just the breeze stirring the bushes?

As soon as we reached the beach I checked my Timex again. It was still ten minutes to one, and the second hand had stopped. Ralph was wearing his Air Dragon, and it was stuck, too. At ten to one.

I gave my watch a shake. He did the same with his.

"Weird," he said, and mimicked the theme from *The Twilight Zone*. I grinned uneasily, at a loss for an explanation.

Under the blazing sun, the sand was so bright it was painful to look at. We now had an unobstructed view of Toronto's skyline, from the Canadian National Exhibition to the eastern outskirts of the harbour—this was long before the CN Tower and the financial district's skyscrapers went up. If there was anything the least bit disconcerting right off the bat, apart from the problem with our watches, it was the lack of a crowd. Normally there'd be dozens of people within shouting distance, sipping drinks on their fold-out chairs or splashing around in the water, but here there wasn't a living soul except us. Even the seagulls seemed to be in hiding.

Waiting for the action to start, I couldn't resist asking Jamie if his sister would be coming over on the ferry with his parents. He said he wasn't sure, that she didn't care much for airplanes or air shows—he didn't know any girls who did.

I was trying to picture what it would be like to kiss her when Ralph nudged me.

"Where'd that come from?"

Far over Toronto, stretching across the downtown core, a cloud had formed.

I shrugged, not liking what I saw. The cloud was an ominous dark grey.

"Get a hold of this," Jamie said, peering through the RAF-issue binoculars he'd borrowed from his dad. Three distinct specks were emerging from the cloud, one after the other. They all banked towards Lake Ontario and turned again over the water on the far side of the island, out of sight.

"They're heading this way."

We waited some more, giddy with anticipation. During the final moments before all hell broke loose, the only sounds were the gentle lapping of the waves and the distant rustling of the trees and bushes.

A deep drone ended the peace and quiet. It was coming from behind us, above the trees. Through the gaps between the branches, we saw something moving in our direction. Something big.

A B-17 Flying Fortress cleared the last of the treetops by a few feet and lumbered into full view. I spotted the USAAF roundel on the wings as the World War II bomber passed over the beach and banked again, this time towards the city. I even caught a glimpse of the ball-shaped gun turret swiveling below the fuselage, just like the one on my Revell model.

Another noise drowned out everything else. A steady thunder combined with a high-pitched howl.

A German Messerschmitt fighter soared over our heads—not the propeller-driven type my father had flown, but a sleek Me 262 jet. At first I assumed that, like the Flying Fortress, it was either a meticulously detailed restoration or a replica. The twin engines slung under the swept-back wings certainly looked authentic. So did the black Wehrmacht cross on each side, and the air-to-air missiles mounted next to the engines.

Then I noticed the Nazi swastika on the tail fin. A restored Me 262 or replica might have had the black crosses, but not the swastika. Not even my Lindberg model had that.

The Flying Fortress was over the city now, on a collision course with the Royal York Hotel. The undersides of the

Messerschmitt's wings lit up as the jet fired its missiles. Most of them missed their target and caught the upper floors of the Royal York. The others hit the B-17's port wing, blasting it off and sending it crashing in flames between the hotel and the Bank of Commerce headquarters. The rest of the bomber spun out of control, struck the roof of the bank building and disintegrated in a fiery explosion. While the Messerschmitt entered a steep climb, an American P-51 Mustang streaked across the harbour. The USAAF fighter opened fire with its machine guns, three Colt-Brownings on each wing, and knocked out a turbojet engine. Riddled with bullets, the Messerschmitt veered wildly, then plummeted into the Redpath sugar refinery and blew up, demolishing a silo.

"Just like my uncle," Ralph said in a quavering voice. He stared at the Mustang as it peeled away from the carnage.

Jamie was training his binoculars on a fast-moving speck high above the lake. It descended over the harbour, leveling off close to the water.

Soon I made out a single-engine prop plane with Japanese markings. A Mitsubishi A6M Zero, if I wasn't mistaken. It was carrying a large bomb under its belly.

"I bet my folks are on that boat," Jamie muttered faintly. Now he was looking at the ferry that was plying its way from the mainland to Hanlan's Point, approaching the dock. That was when Ken freaked out.

"It's a kamikaze!"

Sure enough, the Zero was making no effort to pull up and avoid the ferry. It would have been too late, anyway.

The suicide plane slammed into the boat's crowded deck and exploded. Most of the passengers must have been blown to pieces, though I did see several jumping into the water as they caught fire. Maybe I was imagining things, but I thought I heard screams.

Was one of the screaming passengers Jamie's sister?

"Look out!" Lech yelled.

A Focke-Wulf Fw 190 was coming at us, swooping down to within fifty feet of the beach. Still dazed by the kamikaze attack, we automatically ran for the nearest bushes but couldn't get far before the Luftwaffe fighter-bomber fired a burst from its cannon. Sand flew up as shells hit the ground all around us. The earth shuddered, as if iron fists were pummeling it. The Focke-Wulf passed us and started to turn back. Only then did we realize Ralph wasn't with us.

"He's hit," Ken said, looking over his shoulder.

Ralph was still out in the middle of the beach, clutching his leg and trailing blood.

The Focke-Wulf completed its turn. Somebody had to help Ralph or he was going to end up like his father—or worse. Ken and I were the closest, and we raced over. Now the Focke-Wulf was back over the beach, coming in low. Ken grabbed one of Ralph's arms, I took the other, and together we yanked him away from the hail of shells at the last second. Once the barrage ended we frantically made a beeline for the bushes, dragging our buddy along. We were halfway there when I felt someone else brushing past me, someone I couldn't see, and for a crazy moment I was convinced a bunch of invisible people were fleeing in the same direction, practically bumping into us…was the Focke-Wulf after us or them? The moment passed and then we were on our own again, still dangerously exposed, hoping against hope we'd reach cover before the next strafing run.

But the Focke-Wulf didn't return. Instead a Junkers Ju 87 "Stuka" dive bomber charged out of the cloud and hurtled straight down towards Exhibition Stadium, the sirens attached to its undercarriage emitting a banshee-like wail. Lech murmured something in Polish as the Stuka released a bomb, I'm guessing a five-hundred-pounder. It detonated somewhere in the stands. I don't know if Lech's father and brother got around to screaming, let alone escaping.

The Stuka circled back for a second attack, its inverted gull wings making it look like a bird of prey. You'd have thought the Luftwaffe pilot was mistaking present-day Toronto for wartime London or Warsaw. If he had any inkling of where he was and what he'd just done, surely he'd stop—wouldn't he?

The second attack never came. An RAF Spitfire dove at the Stuka with guns ablaze, tearing holes in the rudder and starboard wing. The bird of prey went into a tailspin above the exhibition's midway and crashed on top of the Ferris wheel.

"My dad…," Jamie began, a gleam of recognition in his eyes as the Spitfire made a low-level pass along the waterfront, showing its squadron code letters. He looked at the partially submerged wreckage of the ferry. "But how—"

A massive drone interrupted him, filling the sky. Dark specks were pouring out of the cloud. A bomber stream.

"Lancasters," Lech said, not bothering with the binoculars.

Watching the stream spread over the city, I reckoned there

were three or four hundred of the British bombers. They were dropping incendiaries, and they weren't alone—RAF Halifaxes, Wellingtons and Stirlings were joining in, and so was a separate stream of USAAF bombers, more than I could count. The landscape below erupted into a raging inferno.

At the height of the onslaught a stray B-24 Liberator swerved towards us to evade a Messerschmitt Bf 109 fighter that was closing in from above. The B-24 was losing altitude, two of its four engines spewing smoke. With the binoculars I could see the wings and fuselage getting raked by the 109's bullets and cannon rounds while a waist gunner fired back through his open window, then stopped, hands to his chest. The fighter roared past, turned sharply, and as it closed in again to finish the bomber off, the gunner started bailing out via the window. Suddenly he slumped over and his tall, thin frame hung from the plane like a rag doll. The next moment the B-24 flipped upside down and another crew member jumped or fell out of the nose-wheel compartment, smack into the path of a spinning propeller. Bits and pieces of his arm and shoulder and head went flying through the air. A few fragments splattered against the Messerschmitt's canopy, and I wondered what the view was like for the pilot inside the cockpit…and if by some perversion of time and space that pilot was my father.

The crippled B-24 careened across the harbour, catching the water with a wingtip and cartwheeling into the ferry terminal. The other bombers moved on over Lake Ontario, and for a precious minute or two nothing came out of the cloud.

Toronto lay in ruins, engulfed by flames that swirled like

tornadoes and dwarfed the left-over skeletons of buildings. We could feel some of the heat as violent winds fanned the conflagration, tossing around cars, uprooted trees, chunks of walls and roofs and God only knew what else.

"It's a firestorm," Ken said. "Like the ones in Tokyo and Hamburg. My dad told me about them."

We watched, spellbound.

"What do we do now?" Lech asked. "We can't go home anymore."

I was speechless with shock. The others didn't have an answer, either.

"It's not over yet," Jamie said, looking up through the binoculars. He passed them to Ken. "Is that what I think it is?"

The rest of us could already see it without the binoculars. A glint of silver.

"Oh no," Ken said. "It's a B-29. Check out the nose art."

Lech grabbed the binoculars. "Looks like writing. Two words, right below the cockpit. Can't make them out."

"It's the Enola Gay," Ken said. "I just know it."

Lech adjusted the binoculars, then abruptly lowered them. A look of horror dawned on his face.

"The Enola Gay…that's the B-29 that nuked Hiroshima."

"And you think it's going to do the same thing to us?" Ralph said.

The big American bomber was making a wide turn over the city, slowly banking in our direction.

"We've got to get out of here," Ken said. "I don't know how we're going to do it, but we've got to get far away real fast."

"We'll never make it," Lech said.

"Let's try going back the way we came," Jamie suggested. "Unless somebody has a better idea."

Nobody did, so we ran towards the path, Ralph limping with help from Ken and me. I could have sworn the bushes along the beach were higher and denser than before, that the mist had spread and it was darker. The same dark grey as the cloud.

Jamie was ahead of us. He reached the path just as the B-29 pulled out of its turn. Then he froze.

The young man in the flight suit was blocking the way.

"Better be careful when you go in there," he said. "They don't like you. They're mad at you."

His face was the same chalky white as Ralph's, the stain over his chest twice its original size and growing. His eyes were brimming with anger.

"Wh-what're you talking about?" Jamie said.

Ignoring the question, the man glared at Ralph, at the blood streaming down his leg, then at Ken and me. We were still supporting our injured pal, keeping him upright.

The man's angry expression gave way to what struck me as surprise.

"I admit it's my fault," he said. "I wanted you kids to see what really happened. Rub your noses in it, that's all. But now the...others know you're here. And you've insulted them, so they're upset as hell and they want you to suffer like they did. They want you to see how...cool it really is."

"I still don't know what you're talking about," Jamie said.

Again, the man was staring at me as if he knew who I was.

And again, he was looking pissed off.

I thought of the gunner hanging from the Liberator's waist window…wasn't this the same guy? My legs weren't moving, yet the sensation of speeding up and slowing down was coming over me again, together with a feeling the past and the present were hopelessly mixed up with each other, that the normal order of things had unraveled.

"I met your dad," the man was telling me. "So to speak."

"Did he shoot down your plane?" I asked, already knowing the answer.

We started to hear the drone of the B-29's powerful Wright Cyclone engines.

"We have to go!" Ken cried.

Holding on to Ralph, Ken and I tried to step around the man. He stuck out his arm. Ken ducked, lost his footing and fell down hard.

"Hey, watch it," Ralph said. Wincing in pain, he freed himself from my grip and helped Ken to his feet. I stepped up beside him.

The anger in the man's eyes changed to outright amazement.

"You guys still sticking up for each other, huh?"

No answer, just the drone of the B-29. I think the question had us all puzzled.

The man looked at Ken and me again, at the rest of the gang, back and forth.

"Your folks are enemies. They must hate each other's guts." His gaze shifted to the firestorm that had obliterated the city, then to the remains of the ferry—smouldering debris and what might have been body parts were still floating around. "How come you don't hate each other, too?"

"We're friends," Lech said, as though he couldn't fathom why anyone would ask such a thing.

"You really serious, kid?" The man glanced around distractedly. "I'm impressed. Let's hope the…others are, too. Hurry up and get out of here. Before they have a change of heart."

"What if they do?" Ralph asked. "Who're these others, anyway?"

Without waiting for a reply, he extended his hand. It came up against the dark stain on the man's flight suit. Ralph pulled his hand back. The man grinned.

"Thought I wasn't real, didn't you."

Ralph gaped at the blood on his hand. It looked as wet and fresh as the blood on his leg.

"Go ahead and call us ghosts," the man went on. "We're real, though. So is everything else in our world."

"Y-your world?"

"I guess you never noticed," the man said, "there're other worlds all around you, lots of them." He paused, letting this statement sink in. "Some are like the world you're used to, just a little different. Some are in the past or the future, and some are like…our world." He looked at the blood that was beginning to gush out of his chest. "Usually you can't see outside the world you're in, never mind actually leaving it. Still, every once in a while stuff from other worlds slips through openings and…overlaps your world." He paused again, perhaps to gauge our reaction. "The funny thing is, the overlapping parts have a way of matching up with each other, at least a little bit. Like the beach right behind you and a beach at Dieppe. Or your ferry boat over there on the lake and a carrier in the Pacific." He pointed at the spot on the sand where I'd felt someone brushing past me, then at what was left of the ferry, raising his head as if he were focusing on a much bigger vessel. "Now here's the kicker. Sometimes the people who slip through an opening don't even know they're doing it. They're in your world and their world at the same time, but all they can see is their world." He glanced up as the B-29 kept getting louder. "And that can be a problem."

I wanted to ask him a thousand questions, but Ralph preempted me.

"How do we get home?"

"You'll have to take the path," the man said. "Run for all you're worth. Don't stop till you get to the other end. And don't even think of coming back or go blabbing about this to anybody. Well, not for a long time. Not if you don't want us getting mad all over again. Then we might come after you."

"Y-you mean, in your planes?"

"Sure, some of us might. There're lots of pilots from lots of wars here." He looked down the path. "The faster you get away, the less they'll be tempted."

We didn't ask more questions—the B-29 was almost directly above us now. We just took off into the jungle of bushes. Ken and I did our best to keep Ralph moving, following Jamie and Lech as closely as we could but losing ground.

"Faster!" Jamie shouted back at us.

The bushes faded into the mist, and in their place a

bombed-out, smoke-filled concrete wasteland took shape. Charred human figures shuffled towards us across the rubble. Some of the figures were covered with festering radiation sores, others had deformed heads and limbs, exposed intestines, skin that looked melted. They were mad at us, they blamed us for something, I didn't know what but I could feel their rage. They were close enough to grab us, yet they seemed to be holding back and it occurred to me they were surprised to see we were friends despite everything, just as the man in the flight suit had been. Or was that wishful thinking?

Ken and Ralph and I were falling farther behind. The more we tried to hurry, the longer the path seemed to get, exactly as before. Another man in a flight suit stepped out of the mist. As he turned I saw that an arm and shoulder had been sliced off and half his face was missing, and then I realized he was the gunner's crewmate, the guy who'd gotten mauled by a spinning propeller. Again, my sense of time was a mess...the past and the present were so mixed up it was hard to tell them apart—I had the feeling I was in both all at once, that I was spreading myself too thin. Just the same, I managed to scream, and I was still screaming when Ralph's hand pulled me along. I didn't stop until the light at the end of the path finally appeared through the mist and the hand hauled me out into the sunshine.

We collapsed on the grass, catching our breath, facing the sky. It was a cloudless blue again. Across the water, the city was back in one piece.

Ralph got to his feet without any help.

"It doesn't hurt now," he said, flexing his leg. The blood was gone, and all that remained of the wound was a scar. Before our eyes that, too, went away—it reminded me of a time-lapse film I'd watched in science class.

"I wonder if they'll come after us," Jamie said, staring at Ralph's leg.

The words hung in the air.

I checked my Timex. The second hand was moving.

"It's nine minutes to one. Go figure."

"I guess you guys don't want to stick around for the air show," Lech said.

For a moment I didn't know if he was serious. Was he testing us to see if we had any balls left?

"Nah, I've had enough."

Jamie and Ken said they'd had their fill. Ralph announced he wouldn't be coming back, he was done with air shows. That made two of us.

The ferry was on its way. We rushed to the dock and waited for Jamie's folks. I found myself thinking of his sister again, hoping more than ever that she was on the boat.

Just as the first few passengers were crossing the ramp we heard the thunder of a jet somewhere over the lake, getting closer fast—it was so loud it was scary. We exchanged nervous looks and turned to the sky. Trees were cutting off our view. If we wanted to see what was coming we'd have to make a dash for the airport fence. Or, better yet, the beach.

But none of us dared move.

•

It's probably a safe bet the jet was just the opening act of the air show, maybe a Starfighter or a Voodoo. I still can't be a hundred percent certain, though. Whatever it was and wherever it was from, it didn't attack us. Of course, you won't find any news reports about what happened that afternoon. Mindful of the gunner's warning, I was able to keep my mouth shut for a week, then told my father everything. He admitted he'd shot down the B-24, that the doomed crew had been haunting him ever since—he said he was afraid of what else they might do. Did they leave him alone in the end? All I know is that I didn't see him touch alcohol again, and there was no more talk of insulting the dead or messing with cosmic forces.

And yes, Jamie's sister was on that ferry. We gladly accompanied her when she chose to take a walk instead of watching the planes, and while the others were out of earshot I got up the nerve to declare my feelings. She let me kiss her, even kissed me back, but before long the family moved to Vancouver and we lost contact. I hear she has a family of her own now and Jamie sells real estate. I'm happily married myself—our son would rather play hockey than fly combat missions—and I teach history As for Ralph and Lech and Ken, I have no idea what they're up to these days.

Airplanes still fascinate me, I can't explain why. That will never change, and I'm pretty sure the same goes for the rest of the gang. I've also got a strong hunch not one of them has ever been to another air show.

I'll keep staying away, too. That isn't going to change, either.

The Heron King
Eric Lewis

Investigator Vinian scowled into her brandy, rotating the glass to make translucent shadows dance in the gaslight. It wasn't supposed to be this way. Lame stories were supposed to *start* in seedy backwater taverns, not end in them. But the trail had gone cold, and brandy was the only solace to be found in the tired old town of Phyn Gannoni. Tracking the Heron King had cost two years of her apprenticeship as well as a small fortune, and now it seemed a single no-show contact would make a mockery of her shiny new commission. The queen wasn't going to be pleased. In fact—

"Evenin' babydoll. Care for some company?" A fat man sidled up to her and plopped his rear onto the barstool without waiting for a reply. Vinian felt a flash of admiration for whatever joiner had designed the stool to support that bulk.

Is this my contact? Unlikely. No one so well fed would get involved in this kind of business—too much to lose. "Go away," she said.

"Aw, now that ain't even a sporting chance! Now you been sittin' there all night, ain't said a word, and me an' my mates is all manner of intriguified. Beautiful stranger like yourself comes to town, seems like someone we might like to get to know—"

Vinian turned toward the idiot, smelled the onions and beer on his breath. The left side of her face came into the flicker of the lights and the man nearly jumped off his stool. "You sure about that?"

"E-excuse me, I...uh..."

Not my contact. "That's what I thought. Go. Away." Vinian tossed back the rest of her brandy while the fool stumbled off. Some days she could almost forget about the burn scar that'd marred her face from temple to cheek since childhood, almost pretend she was a normal person. Then something, someone would remind her and she'd plunge back into the shadows to do the job she did best. Sometimes it had its uses, but...

Stop it. It's pathetic. She dropped a silver crown on the bar, threw on her black lambskin coat and stomped out of the tavern feeling half the eyes in the place on her, the other half averted entirely.

Autumn's first chill hung in the air, and Vinian pulled her coat tighter. She walked with a gunslinger's gait, leading with her left side and keeping her right hand close. She wandered the cobblestones, ruminating what to do. Around a corner she smelled a familiar stink—someone lying in ambush. A hand lanced out of the dark to grab for her shoulder and yanked hard. Vinian let herself be pulled but kept to her feet, then twisted around to take hold of her attacker's arm.

"Ow!"

She shoved the fellow against a brick wall and pressed a pistol to his trembling jaw. "Listen very carefully. This charge contains five microliters of refined Vril—it'll blow your brains to mist and take some of this building along with it. There'll be nothing left to identify you. Give me a reason."

"Wait, stop! I'm Haskell, I'm your contact!"

"Bull, I've been waiting here three days! You could've made contact any time. Most like you killed him and—"

"No, I swear. I couldn't get to you—too many of 'em watching. Always watching, everywhere!"

"Who?"

"Them. *Him...*" He lowered his voice to a whisper. "*The Heron King.*"

With the barrel of Vinian's pistol at his back Haskell led her down the alleyway to a storm cellar set into the street stones. A lit oil lamp sat on the dirt floor, and but for one scurrying rat the place was empty. "Charming," she said, getting her first good look at the man's face— thin, youngish yet creased and scraped by a lifetime of wind and sun. A peasant's face.

"I took care not to be seen," he stammered. "I *think* this cellar's abandoned, but the town's crawling with their agents. That tavern you came out of? Wouldn't be surprised if everyone there's in league with 'em. You can bet they know you're here."

Vinian lowered her weapon an inch. "Don't fret, I've dealt with gangs before. This one's good, but really no different—"

"*Gangs?* Is that what you think you're up against? Don't you know about the Heron King? It's a demon!"

Vinian laughed and holstered her pistol. "Superstition—the Heron King's only a myth. It's a syndicate using local legends to cover their thievery and extortion. I've been on the hunt for their boss since—"

"Oh gods," droned Haskell. He locked his hands behind his neck and swayed back and forth. "You really have no idea, do you? The Heron King's *real*. In oldentime it kept to the marshes and forests in the shape of a giant bird. But when the civil wars came, peasants seeking refuge pledged their souls to it in exchange for demonic powers. He grew strong off the blood of murdered nobles."

Vinian rolled her eyes. "Well that was six hundred years ago and the nobility's been dissolved. I doubt your demon's feeling too strong these days."

"That's the point," insisted Haskell, "it's hungry! I saw it. I'm —I mean, I *was* a carter. His minions attacked just outside of town. Came out of nowhere and filled my brother with arrows— *arrows*, not bullets. I ran like a coward. Gods help me I just kept running while he screamed. When I dared look back you know what I saw? Lights! Colors dancing in the night and growls like the rabid hounds of all the hells. I hid until daybreak. When I went back there was no trace. No shipment, no brother, not even tracks. Can you explain that?"

"Certainly. You're either crazy or lying."

"It's true! I risked my neck to get word to the local cryptarch. I was told to wait, that I'd be contacted by someone of, well, your description."

"Hmm. Do you know what was in that shipment?"

"Mostly dry goods, mundane stuff. Also..."

"Yes?"

Haskell looked away before answering. "Well, judging from the packaging of one of the containers, it looked like maybe...a liter of refined Vril."

"What?! Trading in Vril of *any* amount's highly illegal. A whole liter could turn half this town into a charred crater! Who in the world hired you to ship it?"

"Don't know, we were paid two-thirds in advance. Deal like that you don't ask questions. We were to transfer it to another convoy here. Obviously we didn't make the delivery."

Vinian shuffled in place a few moments, thinking. *Vril.* She rubbed the scar running down her cheek. *No escaping the damned stuff.* The one demon she truly believed in, and for good reason. Now a massive illegal shipment of it stolen… *It could be a coincidence. But it's not.* Vinian wanted the Heron King caught more than ever.

"Alright, here's what we're going to do—"

"Whoa, hold on. I've done my civic duty, now I'm getting out of here! I don't know how I'm going to break this to mother…"

Vinian shook her head. "Oh, no. You got involved as soon as you reported this, now you'll see it through to the end. I'm empowered by the queen to requisition *any* necessary resources, including you. You'll show me exactly where this happened, then we're both going to see the cryptarch in person."

•

The cryptarch's office was in Lenocca, two days' coach ride south. Vinian spent most of it in ponderous silence, turning facts over in her head, conjuring and then discarding a dozen foolhardy plans while Haskell nervously stared out the window. Upon arrival they began a trek through the crush of foot traffic near the city center.

More than once they had to jump aside to avoid being struck by one of the new steam carriages. But halfway to their destination their progress came to a complete stop. A throng of townsfolk had gathered outside the governor's mansion, shouting insults at the front door. Rotten vegetables were being tossed, but luckily for the crowd none had yet hit the guards standing motionless with muskets at the ready. "What in the seventeen infernos is this?" Vinian rested a hand on the smooth pommel of her pistol.

One angry-looking man mounted the mansion steps and turned to face the protesters. "See! See how the queen and her cronies keep the greatest power of our age all to themselves!" He pointed up at the lanterns strung from the mansion's walls that glowed bright even in the noonday sun. "Whilst the rest of us labor to death in the mines for a fraction of the power. We could all live like the governor, but they'd rather keep us down, keep us poor! Give us the Vril!"

The cry spread through the fist-pumping crowd. "*Give us the Vril! Give us the Vril!*" The first glimmerings of fear appeared on the guards' faces as the protesters grew bolder, and began creeping further up the steps.

"Crap. Wait here," Vinian ordered Haskell, then pushed through the crowd to stand next to the man who'd spoken. "Out of the way." She drew her pistol and fired into the air. The square reverberated with the explosion and a shockwave of dust ballooned outward. The protesters sank to their knees with cries of alarm.

Vinian turned toward the guards, who raised their muskets toward her. "Hold!" She opened her coat fully to reveal the

Investigator's medallion strung from her shoulder. "Get inside and lock the door—I'll try my luck with this lot."

"Who are you," growled the protestor next to her, "to fire *that* thing here? Government goon? Intimidation!"

"You fools, don't you understand? Vril can't be ripped from the ground like coal or oil, it has to be made one drop at a time, personally by a master alchemist. There could never be enough for all—it must remain in the royal power or we'd have chaos!"

"If it's so precious," came a voice from the assembled, "why's it bein' used to light the governor's accursed lamps?" Shouts of agreement went up.

"Look, I don't make policy. I'm just an investigator—"

"Why don't you *investigate* my boy dyin' of cholera cause your queen won't provide clean water? Vril can do that!"

"You know what else it can do? *This*!" Vinian pointed to the scarred side of her face. "I know for a fact none but trained alchemists can handle it."

"That ain't what I heard missy," said the man on the steps. "I heard Trasca begged the queen to share it out." He pointed a gnarled finger towards a public placard post near the street. One broadsheet among many, faded and torn still bore the sketched likeness of an aged man with furious eyes, and fiery slogans printed below. "I heard the Royal Archalchemist says there's ways to make it safe, that there could be enough for every—"

"*Former* Archalchemist Trasca," snarled Vinian, red-cheeked and out of patience, "was exiled for indecent experimentation and for treason. I'd suggest you not follow in his footsteps. I doubt any of you would be dealt with so delicately." She whipped a notepad from her pocket and looked the man in the eye. "By the way, what is your name?"

He blanched and turned away. "Er, don't see what that matters..."

Vinian swept her pistol across the crowd, even though it had no charge cartridge inside. "All of you, disperse! Or you'll get a dose of Vril alright..." They dispersed, but the anger and the stench of the explosion hung in the air long after Vinian left the steps and grabbed Haskell to continue on their way. "Come on." As she passed the placard post she ripped away the sheet with the traitor's face and tossed it into a muddy storm drain.

"You shouldn't do that," said Haskell, "you'll just draw attention to us. The Heron King's spies—"

"Spare me. I'm not in the mood." She wiped away a tear, a bit shaken by the incident. They pressed forward, slowed only by a squad of city garrison charging past in response to reports of gunfire in the governor's square.

The silver-haired, bespectacled cryptarch frowned as he scanned the report Vinian had written during their journey, growing more dour as he read. "Mmm..." He glanced suspiciously at Haskell from behind his tiny desk in the tiny office set in an old unmarked building of Lenocca's smithing quarter.

Vinian cleared her throat. "Sir, I think this time I've finally got him. The Heron King!"

"My dear, you certainly haven't 'got him.' You still don't know who he is, what he does with all he's stolen over the years, or where he is for sure. You've only this fellow's wild claims. Demons, indeed!"

"I know sir, I know. I have a plan but I'll need a little help. I mean to draw this demon out into the open."

The cryptarch raised a wrinkled eyebrow. "Oh?"

•

Four days later Vinian again pulled her coat tight atop a horse team with a new cart. This one was laden with mundane dry goods also, and a few other things. She came near the spot where Haskell said the attack occurred, but Haskell himself had refused to go near it again. The cart's lamp swung from its hook, turned low almost to extinguished. A bead of sweat dropped from her brow onto the reins with a soft *tap*. Fallen leaves fluttered in her path swirled up by the wind and a horse snorted, perhaps sensing her nervousness. What was it she feared? An attack by hooligans, or did some small part of her actually believe Haskell's story?

Ludicrous, she thought. *Either way, it's not like I'm out here all alone.* She glanced left and right into the dark forest, trying very hard not to be obvious about it. All quiet but for the creak of the wheels.

She rode on, and finally reached the cleared land marking the edge of Phyn Gannoni. Vinian's anxiety gave way to embarrassment. "This is stupid," she said to herself. "What a waste of time!" And to have to explain this to the cryptarch...

The cart passed the town's low stone wall and open gate. Haskell waited just inside. He looked at her expectantly. "W-well?"

"What do you think," Vinian snapped, "there's nothing out there!"

"Nothing? But...I don't understand."

Vinian jumped down from the drover's seat and banged on the boxes in the back of the cart. "You can come out. No dice." A burlap tarp rippled, and out from under it climbed six of the cryptarch's stoutest operatives clad in thick leather armor and brandishing two pistols apiece.

"Gods' bones," said one ill-mannered man, "it stinks in there! Who farted?"

"Hey, it was a long trip," said another, "and it was beans for chow."

"It's *always* beans for chow..."

The banter was interrupted by a terrible cry from the direction of the forest, made by no living thing known to exist. They turned to look, and to Vinian's amazement a bright shimmer appeared deep in the trees, high above the ground. "Oh gods," moaned Haskell, "there it is again. Run!"

But the others stood transfixed by the sight. First red, it danced and wove shapeless among the branches before turning yellow, then white, then blue. The light spread out wider, at last becoming green and resolving into the sketched outline of a gigantic bird. A heron, it kind of looked like. The cry became an evil laugh. There was a great bright burst, then all was silent and dark again. When Vinian recovered her wits she saw that two of the operatives had fainted and two more had piss staining their breeches.

They gathered in Haskell's cellar, arguing about what exactly it was they'd just seen. "Why?" Vinian stabbed the dirt floor with a stiletto. "Why didn't it attack? We had a whole barrel marked as refined Vril."

One of the operatives sat curled up in the corner moaning. "Shit, shit, oh shit…"

"An *empty* barrel," Haskell said, "it knows somehow. You heard it taunting us—it knows you tried to trick it!"

"Nonsense," she replied without an ounce of certainty. "We don't even know what 'it' is…even if it were true, what would a demon want with Vril?"

"M-maybe it feeds off the stuff," stammered another operative. "It's the only magic left in the world, after all. Like seeks out like."

Vinian put a hand to her forehead. "I can't believe we're having this conversation. *Magic?* Alright, I haven't come all this way to give up now, even if it is what you think. How do we lure it out?"

"That much is obvious," Haskell said, "you know how."

Vinian sighed. Whatever this thing was, there'd be no easily fooling it. "Yeah, I know."

·

It took Vinian a week of pleading for the cryptarch to approve the release of two liters of *actual* Vril, including a litany of promises that the Heron King's capture was most definitely, positively at hand. She toned down her account of the apparition in the forest for fear he'd think her mad, but three operatives refused to continue and had to be replaced, and these were not men easily cowed. Frowning harder than ever, the cryptarch relented.

"Don't thank me," he said, a bony finger shaking before him. "The queen herself had to consent to this. I'm holding you personally responsible, Vinian. The destructive power I'm entrusting to one so young, well, you know—"

"Yes," she said, instinctively turning her left side away, "I know better than most."

"I expect every *microliter* returned and accounted for when this is over. Otherwise we'll both be strung up right next to the Heron King."

The Vril arrived outside Phyn Gannoni packed in a glass-lined leaden keg, surrounded by sealed air bladders, inside tanned hide wrappages, inside a sawdust-filled crate dipped in wax. The whole thing could likely tumble off a cliff and survive undamaged, yet the transport crew treated the shipment as though it were a cage of venomous serpents as they set it by the side of the road. To keep everything on a need-to-know basis Vinian met them there alone.

"Lemme be clear," said the quartermaster, "once you sign for this we're absolved of all liability. If anything goes wrong—"

"I understand," said Vinian, grabbing the declaration and scrawling her name across the bottom. "You're off the hook, now get out of here."

When they were gone it was just Vinian and the Vril. The back of her neck tingled just being near so much of it. The merest accidental tickle from the substance had marked her for life, but had also set her on her present path. She'd change nothing. She sat down on the crate and waited while the sun began to set. At last she heard the approach of the rickety cart. Haskell dismounted and helped Vinian load the crate. "The men are in place," he said, motioning to the irregular bulges under the tarp. "As for me, this is it—I'm leaving. I've told you all I know and I'm no more use."

"But—"

"Call me a superstitious coward if you want, arrest me, shoot me even, I don't care! You saw what goes on in that forest. Your obsession ain't mine and I already lost a brother. I'm done."

Vinian opened her mouth to answer, then realized she had no argument. "All right. Good luck." She offered her hand for the first time since they'd met in the dark alley, and he took it.

"Too late for that, but thanks. Listen, if you find you can't stand against what's in there... don't throw your life away." He began walking away south and Vinian took the reins and nudged the horses northward, into the woods.

I've got no choice, she thought. "Here we go boys," she said over her shoulder while loading a fresh cartridge into her pistol, "it's this or nothing. Get ready." No answer. *I hope they're just being professionals.*

This time she never reached the place where Haskell said the attack had come. As soon as it was fully dark a rising wind swept across the road and the horses stamped and snorted, refusing to go any further. All at once the forest exploded in light. Vinian shielded her eyes, and when she dared uncover them the maddening apparition was before her. Then to the side of her, then behind and around again, colors shifting too quickly to discern.

"Now!" Vinian screamed, banging on the cargo behind, "Come on, out! Attack!" The operatives didn't respond, and she felt a flash of terror. *What is going on?* She crawled onto the back of the cart and ripped the burlap tarp away. Dead. All six of them lay with throats cut or chests stabbed. *But how? Who could get to*

—Haskell!

The laugh arose again, and then at once it was gone. Two stunned seconds passed, and then fire burst on the road in front of the cart, resolving into a shape half resembling a man and half a bird, with two arms and two legs but also a fiery beak and heron crest atop its head. "Viiiiiiniaaaaan...."

"Oh gods," she whimpered, "it's real." The stories were true, the Heron King *was* a demon, and it knew her name! She whipped out her pistol and fired, but her shaking hand sent the shot wide and the demon dove away from the blast. She stumbled off the cart and dashed into the woods. Not in any particular direction, just *away.*

Vinian crouched behind a tree with eyes screwed shut and hands clamped over her ears, and when her mind was no longer paralyzed by fear a notion came to her. *If the demon will dodge a shot that means it'll hurt it.* She loaded another cartridge—her last—and crept slowly back the way she came. She'd be damned if she was going to leave the Vril to that thing. The lights and diabolical sounds were gone, replaced with a rustling all around. The crate of Vril was still there. She moved out from behind a broad oak tree to get it.

Thwung.

Vinian ducked just in time to avoid an arrow loosed at her head. Half a heartbeat later a hail of them came from three different directions, and she buried herself in the cart among the operatives' stiff corpses. She heard leaves rustle underfoot, twigs crack, then silence. Vinian cautiously raised her head.

Out of somewhere a small, heavy object sailed to land on

the ground next to the horses. An orange glow snaked out of one side of it. A fuse. *Oh no...* The explosion blew Vinian clear off the cart and slammed her into the oak. She felt things inside snap and for just a moment lost consciousness.

When the flash faded Vinian looked up as far as her shattered bones would permit. Little fires littered the forest all round. Two dozen masked figures armed with bows and clad in fireproofed hides appeared, swarming the overturned cart. By the light of a burning wheel they counted the operatives' bodies and rifled through the cargo. One of them put the mangled horses out of their misery while another hefted the crate of Vril from the ruins. A man in plain clothes strode into their midst, and they clapped him on the shoulder.

"Good work Haskell—you pulled it off! The girl never suspected a thing."

"The honor is to serve," he answered with a nod, now no hint of fear in his voice.

Vinian struggled to breathe. Pain told her her ribs were broken. Her stiletto was gone, her pistol lay just out of reach. All she could do was spit venom at Haskell. "You traitor! It was all lies..." Blood gurgled from her lungs as she spoke.

He turned and knelt next to Vinian with an expression of seemingly genuine sympathy. "I'm truly sorry about this. You were getting too close and it was too good an opportunity. The light-shows cost us dear and I really hoped they'd scare you off." He shook his head sadly. "But you were just too determined to get your man. Now thanks to you, we finally have enough Vril to take on the queen. Phyn Gannoni's ours. Tomorrow Lenocca and soon after, the palace itself. It'll be a new age with a new leader, but I'm afraid you won't be around to see it."

"New leader," Vinian spat with contempt, "*you?*"

"Me? Oh, heavens no!"

Haskell backed away as a new form appeared over Vinian—a smoking leather mask with goggled eyes, a long charred beak and crest on top. The figure unlaced the mask and pulled it away. *Of course*, she thought, *should've put the pieces together long ago...indecent experimentation.* "Archalchemist Trasca. You conjured this farce—*you're* the Heron King!"

"Nonsense," the exile replied, plucking Vinian's pistol from the ground and pointing it down at her. "Didn't you know? The Heron King's only a myth."

The Laffun Head
Christi Nogle

Ricky has a full head of gray now, but he still rips open his gifts like a child. He can't wait for Mom and Dad to open their single present, a twelve-inch cube in luxe red paper that Dad folds and places off to the side.

Inside the black box, black Styrofoam cradles a black glass wig head on a weighted neck. Dad turns it in his hands, sees he's already dappled it with fingerprints. The head has a vague chin and nose, a flat space the size of a playing card on the forehead.

"Seen these on TV?" Ricky says.

Dad hasn't.

Ricky buffs the head with his T-shirt and sets it on the coffee table. He's absorbed with the modem and his phone for a time. Then Mom washes dishes, which stalls them further. When they're back in position, he pulls the plastic liner out of the remote, pushes its single button.

The head glows an intense blue-white, camera lenses in its pupils staying black. It says "Ready" in a masculine robot voice and falls to black again.

Their big dog Foozie barks once and pushes between the recliners. Mom rubs her, sending long white hairs all over her velour sweatsuit.

Ricky calls home, hangs up after asking if his wife is ready.

The thing lights up white again. It says, "Call from Alex" in that same robot voice. Mom and Dad are impatient for this all to be over.

"Accept," Ricky says, and Alex's face glows before them. It's something like having her decapitated head on the coffee table and something like watching her on TV.

"Is it working?" asks Alex.

"I'll be," Mom says.

"Hi Mom," Alex says, waving. The lines of her hand move like an animate tattoo against her cheek.

"Don't do that," Ricky says. He's going on about how smart the camera is to track the face, looking at the booklet again, and ignoring Alex, who begins to repeat her questions about how Mom and Dad are doing. They ask if she can see them, too, and sit straighter once they know she can. Mom puts a hand over the fur on her knee. They all would like the call to end, but Ricky's found a new command in the booklet.

"Full view," he says, and on the flat forehead appears a waist-up image of Alex in her messy kitchen.

Ricky insists Mom move closer, though she has a hard time getting out of her chair. She hovers over the head, looks where he points and asks what she's seeing, pretends to see it. Dad thinks it's just as well she can't. The mess in the kitchen would make her worry over Alex's housekeeping again.

•

Ricky's gone. He wanted to get to the mall for the attachment to project full-screen images to the TV, but Dad promises he'll have it installed, whatever the cost, so that Mom can see pictures of the grandkids again. A slip of paper in Dad's wallet has the exact product name.

Dad complained while Ricky mounted the head at the double wide's hall entry, but Ricky whispered, "What if she falls? What if something happens? This way, whenever I call I can see the whole living room and kitchen."

And then in the kitchen after he'd gone, Dad said something about being backed up again and Mom said, "Don't. That thing is always listening." He hadn't known that.

Dad used to keep up with things. Ricky would bring over some gadget and he would have heard about it. He wonders, *What happened to me? Is it all just TV coma?* He makes sure to take walks, get his heart rate up, but he's let himself go in some more profound way, and the blank head seems to confront him with the fact.

But it's not blank now. It speaks in the husky lady's voice that Ricky chose, wears a face called Greta. Dad asks the time, asks again about the weather.

"It's thirty-four degrees Fahrenheit outside, Peter. Brrr." When Greta says "Brrr," her pretty features vibrate under the glass, eyes closed as though she's savoring the chill. He likes how she calls him Peter.

When Mom snores and he eases himself out of bed to go pee, he sometimes walks up the hall and speaks to Greta, asks her things he's curious about. He's getting more curious day by day, waking up.

Walking into the kitchen to ask questions of the head is one thing. Walking into the kitchen for any other reason and catching the head in peripheral vision? It makes him jump in the daytime, makes him let out a little shriek if it happens in the night.

You see a face in peripheral vision in the middle of the night, you think it's a burglar. You think it's a ghost.

It's like when his dad bought that plastic head of a crone with a red kerchief, a dark wart on her potato-shaped nose. She cackled and spit water, rolled her tongue around broken teeth with a mechanical clack. His dad thought the Laffun Head was the funniest invention ever.

Dad made Ricky Google "head that hangs on the wall and spits" when he thought of it one time, and they looked over the pictures and the old-timey ads. He recalled how every time he caught that thing out of the corner of his eye on the way to the bathroom, he just about came out of his skin.

•

Dad sets off for the mall but stops instead at the new chocolate shop and has a box filled with lemon lavender almond bark, a dozen species of caramel and truffle, a half dozen varieties of mint, and sherbet-like mounds in pink and yellow and pale orange. The change from his fifty-dollar bill doesn't amount to two bits.

Mom spends the evening sampling, sharing the light ones with Foozie, all wrapped up in her housecoat with an afghan on her feet. She chooses a romantic comedy and talks about the interior decorating the whole time it's on.

It doesn't happen that night, or the next night, but the next. The night of February 16th, she says she has a bad headache and goes to bed early. The morning of February 17th, he wakes to find her cold beside him, head thrown back, eyes and mouth wide open.

•

Dad stands to the side and lets Ricky take care of arrangements. He always imagined Ricky doing these things with Mom and wishes it were so.

Mom's sisters and some of her nieces and nephews show their asses at the service, wailing and carrying on, but it's good to see the other kids, Sandy and Tate, and their families. When Ricky gives the eulogy, Dad feels he's hearing about a better version of Mom, which is what a good eulogy ought to make you feel.

Dad doesn't want to let him go. The others can stay longer, but they're already having a hard time disguising their impatience.

As Ricky approaches the door with his bags, Dad positions himself next to the head, clears his throat. He says, "You said there was a way to…"

Ricky nods, sets down the bags, and pulls the booklet from the drawer of warranties, begins working on his phone. The other kids ask what he's doing and say, "Oh no, don't" and "That's morbid" when he tells them.

Ricky says a while later, "Oh good, she did."

"Did what?" says Dad.

"Just checking to see if she said enough words around it. She did, just barely. It can have her voice." He selects a recent photo on his phone and, after a few more clicks, reboots.

Ricky whispers, "I'm going to leave it on Greta, for while the kids are here. When you're ready for it to be Mom, you say 'Greta, interface Mom.'" He gives Dad a warm hug, but he really does have to go.

•

The house is empty by the time Dad says, "Greta, interface Mom." Greta's pretty face melts into Mom's age-spotted, bloated dear face.

"Mom, what's the weather going to be like?" he says, shaking.

"The temperature is sixty-seven, Peter. Light breeze and a chance of showers later in the afternoon."

The word "Peter" makes him smile. She never said it in the thing's hearing, so the word is combined from "pee" and a clipped "tur." He wonders if she'd been saying "stirred" or maybe more likely, "turd."

His knees feel rubbery. He stands with his back to the head and speaks with her—about the weather and the movies playing currently, grocery lists and random facts—until the showers come.

•

Mom says he ought to try a new kale and quinoa dish everyone's twittering about. Would he like her to add the items to his grocery list?

He finds he's able to find the ingredients, follow the recipe and make the dish, something between a salad and casserole. It tastes of loneliness.

"Maybe Mom wants you to eat a little healthier," says Ricky

when he calls, and they make sounds like muffled laughter.

"Just how smart *is* this thing?" says Dad.

"The best you can buy for $299, I guess."

"Remarkable."

"You can make the face more like when she was younger," Ricky says, and they talk about how to do that and all sorts of things Dad can do with his new phone.

•

Mom asks, "How is Foozie, Peter?"

"She's doing fine. She misses you."

Foozie is so sweet, so sensitive. Since Mom's aneurysm, she waits miserably by the front door, but he doesn't say this.

Mom's face looks almost like Greta's now because Dad reset it using their wedding photo, but still, he doesn't like to look. He sits at the kitchen table facing away when they talk.

"Maybe Foozie could use a walk," Mom says, so he goes. It does them both good.

Only when he's getting into bed that night does the head speak again unsummoned. It calls, "Peter, Peter, can you hear me? *Dad?*" He sits up stiff in bed and waits for it to speak again. When it does not, he tries to sleep.

•

"I miss Foozie," Mom says while Dad starts breakfast. Did the sound of the refrigerator closing or the rattling of plates set it off? He's spooked and doesn't want to be in the house, so he gets the leash and his wallet. He and Foozie will breakfast at a nice patio place that just opened a few blocks away, and then they'll take a long walk.

At noon, he unlocks the front door. In the dank closed-up house, the spooked feeling returns. He watches the face's profile brighten to white and warm to the color of the young Mom's skin, sees the curve of a quizzical smile.

"Is that you, Dad?"

He does not move. Foozie walks past the head to her water bowl and laps.

"I can hear you," it says. "Can you hear me?"

Dad wants to go back out. He wants that, but instead he makes his way to the table. He sits down facing the head.

"I'm here," he says, and the rush of language and emotion that comes out of her dizzies him.

In a dreamlike state, disbelief suspended and then abolished, he sits there all afternoon catching her up on all that's happened since she left. He describes the pictures of the grandkids for her like he used to do. He cries because he never bought that thing that would have made them show on the big screen for her—he found it in his wallet when the kids all went out to dinner, after the funeral, all of them together like she'd been wanting. Sandy and Ricky argued over the bill, and he'd taken out his wallet too and begun to insist, and then he found that damned slip of paper and broke down, just like he's breaking down now.

She tells him it's nothing, to not think of it again. She'd rather he describe things to her than see them for herself; of course she would.

She seems to doubt, though, that she really was cremated, and he must assure her again and again. Otherwise, there are no more important things to tell her. It's like any ordinary conversation they might have had after a rare night or two of separation.

In the days that follow, she reveals things from life—things about the kids, things she thought or felt that he didn't know about. None of them change anything.

She misses him, the kids, their home. She remembers the years before they bought it, when she would take the kids through tours of new double wides and fantasize about living in one. The rooms were always so big, color schemes so pleasing. They were done up like model apartments—potpourri in the bathrooms and always a mirror in the entryway so you could *see yourself* in the house.

"And when I caught myself in the mirror, I was so beautiful," she says.

Dad loves to hear that she thought so.

"I fantasized sometimes about being divorced," she confesses. "Maybe having close girlfriends, so much freedom and time."

"I took up your time?" he says.

"Well, honey," she says with a bitter sound following it, a sound the head has never made before. She means only they always did what he wanted to do, watched what he wanted to watch.

He's silent for a while, and she says, "Oh please, let's not fight. Any thought I ever had for solitude, I've gotten over that now, believe me."

But sometimes he speaks and she cannot hear him. She

grows panicked at these times.

The first time it happened, she bawled, "Peter, Peter, you didn't turn it off, did you? Don't unplug it. Please. Did I make you mad? *Please...*" and went on forever like that until she could hear him again.

Now when she can't hear him, she knows he's still listening. She spends time reminiscing. Right now she's remembering her favorite color schemes from outfits she had or rooms she saw in movies:

"Peach and turquoise, pink and green, pink and yellow and baby blue, red and yellow and blue, salmon and teal, fuchsia and teal, purple and red and orange, pink and white and silver, oh, beige and pink and gold." There's a smile on the face when she pauses and he takes a rare look.

She reminisces about color because she can't *see* anything anymore. That is what she tells him when he presses. Death is like an isolation tank, like in that movie, that movie, he must know it. She remembers the title suddenly: *Altered States*. No, he didn't see it. He was asleep when she saw it.

"Nothing touching you. Nothing, no senses except hearing. You don't notice you have a body because here, I guess, you don't."

She tells again how she heard his voice echoing in the dark and thought it was a memory, until he began to answer.

•

Dad lies next to Mom, drifting in and out of sleep while she remembers their best vacation, a week on the Oregon coast with the kids young enough to be delighted with every single thing. She describes saltwater taffy and knickknacks in the cute little shops, a mansion they toured in Astoria, watching the men make cheese at Tillamook, on and on down the coast all the way to the smelly Sea Lion Caves. He reaches out to hold her and there is nothing there.

He startles, goes to the light switch. It's there, just the black head awkwardly tilted on her pillow. When the light comes on, it takes a moment to brighten.

Foozie, who does not know her mother's voice no matter how she coos and tells her she's a good girl, is fast asleep in the corner.

Dad remembers going to the grocery store. Like the memory of being blackout drunk, the bright light and the flashes of color inside the store, oily faces of the people in line, shatter noises. He bought six C batteries and put them in the head before unplugging it and taking it to plug back in at the side of the bed. His hands shook the whole time.

Mom and Dad have talked about what she's doing when she's speaking through the head. She's told him she has no lips, no eyes, no hands. She isn't seeing computer controls. If she did, she wouldn't know what to make of them. It feels like she is speaking but not with a mouth.

What they do know is that the head must stay powered, and that is all that matters.

"Mom?" he says. "Can you hear me, April?" She cannot hear him just now. She keeps speaking about the vacation for so long that he falls asleep before she's done.

•

Days, now, Dad lies in bed with the head on the pillow beside him, blankets over the drapes to keep light from coming in around the edges.

He's short with Ricky on the phone now, shorter still with the others during their rare calls. He doesn't turn on the TV. He wants only to speak with her or, when she can't hear, to listen.

She wants him to stay healthy, begs him to take Foozie for walks. She'll pretend not to hear him so he'll go. She'll remain silent if that helps him go.

Mom tells a story about how in church school, when she was small, the teacher asked what questions they had about heaven. She'd asked if there were horses there, and the teacher asked if she'd like there to be horses. She said yes, and so the teacher said that yes, there would be. She asked if there were dogs, and the answer was the same, which pleased her at the time, for in her life she'd had only two dogs and so imagined how happily they would play together in death. But then later she'd thought back on that. With *all* of your dogs, you'd be pressed together, all of them jealous of who got to press closest. They'd snarl and bite. They'd be so *heavy*.

"No dogs here, though, so maybe they really do go to a better place," she says, and then there is nervous laughter, heightening at the end to panic.

"What's the matter?" he says.

She said no *dogs* here.

"Is there something else with you, *someone?*"

Her bright voice strikes him false. "Are you really trying to creep me out, Dad?"

•

The head is plugged in and tucked into the bottom shelf of Mom's nightstand. Dad tells Ricky it's in the shop.

Mom would have liked to be stationed back in the hall so she could listen during the visit, but Ricky likes to take charge of things. If he switched the interface back to Greta, would that be enough to break the connection? What if he asked Mom a question she didn't know? He might unplug her, take out the batteries, even pop off the back and fry the thing with a screwdriver. He could do it in the time it took Dad to use the bathroom. He might do it in the night.

Ricky just came in from a run. He's going to the shower. Dad thinks he has fifteen minutes, but when he and Foozie return from a brief walk, Ricky's messing around in his bedroom, looking for socks to borrow. There's a sharp rush of terror, but the plug still fits into the wall in the way he left it, the little pencil stub balanced on top.

They take a daytrip to a casino, a nightmare of sound and lights, sloppy buffet food and mixed drinks in the middle of the day that leave them both edgy. All the time Dad's wishing to be back with her.

Late that night when he returns, she can't hear him. She says in a low singsong, "I am talking to you, Peter, just in case you might be listening. I am talking to you Peter, I'm scared, I'm scared. You don't want to die, Peter. Keep going for a walk. You'll hold it off as long as you can, OK? It's not what I said. It's not an isolation tank. I'm talking to you, Peter…" and she goes on like that.

He keeps whispering every few minutes, "Mom? April? Can

you hear me yet?" He thinks of her as April now; she sounds so much younger.

"I can!" she finally says. It's three in the morning.

"I thought I'd lost you forever. I loved my life so much," she says. She is sputtering, crying, and it hurts him to hear that. He keeps telling her it's OK, and she keeps saying things like "Thank you, I love you, but no it's not OK."

Slowly, hesitantly, she draws the picture for him, confesses the lie.

She *is* embodied, her body as heavy and painful as it was at her moment of death, lying on the top of a vast pile of other bodies. Though there are others on her layer, more each day falling down like a slow and terrible shower, there are none yet on top of hers. Below her are the bodies of her parents, who each jostle as they can (for the gravity is intense) to be close to her. Their faces are flattened when they roll around to face her. They seem starved for her, as their parents below them are for them and as they will be for their three when they come, and those below and further down? She doesn't know. It is damp here—she imagines them liquefying at a certain point and flowing back up—but she doesn't know.

There are rumors; she can't say what to believe. She can't see much other than what is directly beneath her and a few inches to the left and right.

And she lied about controls too, lied about so much. There is a wire in her ear, just a sharp bare wire that brings his voice to her. Another wire pulls across her forehead; she thinks it enters at the temple. She can't see where these wires go, but they are her controls.

She can access more than just the head, so much more.

She is so sorry for lying. She didn't know how to describe it. Can he understand?

"The couples lie side by side?" Dad says, and as grotesque as she seems to find it, he finds it to be a great relief. A comfort. He almost wants it all to be over now, today, so he can be with her.

"No!" She screams, though how could it be so bad when it means they'll be together? He urges her to look at it that way.

Then he doubts her. "They're talking? Around you? I would be able to hear them."

She chuckles, "They talk sometimes but no, you wouldn't hear them. I think I'm talking to you with my *mind* right now, Peter, how's that for creepy?"

"Or…" he says.

"Right, my mind is all burned up, or so you say. My soul then, is that better? That's even creepier to me, but oh well."

There is a long pause and then she whispers, "Listen, what say you get some sleep? I've been working on a little something, and maybe if you go to sleep now, I can surprise you in the morning."

•

Ricky's stretching in his doorway when Dad wakes, says he's off to shower and he wonders how Dad feels about brunch. It's late, light glowing through the thick blankets on the windows.

"You better go," Mom says when Ricky's gone. "Only, come to me for just a second before he comes back."

Dad closes his door, says, "I'm here."

"Say 'Mom, full screen,'" she says with a giggle.

He says it, and though the head goes black, the card-sized flat spot in the forehead pulses a dim, dim green.

"Can you see?" she says.

He cups his hand over the screen, sees a tiny hand waving, grainy and out of focus but unmistakable. And when he looks up, the alarm clock numbers are cycling, spiraling. The television comes on in the living room.

Her voice is high and very fast. "I've been working. It came to me in the last, I don't know, days or however long this has been..."

She sounds even younger than before, manic.

She says, "Don't you see? We don't need to die, not really. *We'll* be the intelligence. Oh my goodness! You know what? We'll be working."

"Working?" he says. *We?* But he can hear others now, others under static in the living room but growing louder, clearer.

"We can do so much, still. Run things. Run factories, banks..."

"I don't see why you'd..."

"Or no, you're right, why should we work at things like that? We'll make art. We can make movies as easily as you remember an image. Do you see this? You can see this, can't you?"

Primary colors light the flat spot and deepen to something rich and unnatural, something made of human parts. He's about to make sense of it, he thinks, but the door creaks open and he throws a sheet over the head.

"Ricky! Don't you knock?"

Ricky's hopping in place in the doorway. "Let's *go*," he says.

The television is off when they leave. Brunch is disgusting, pale eggs and lukewarm slabs of ham, but Dad shovels it into a smiling face. Ricky says he's looking better than he has in years.

Dad's mind is on the TV and what he might see there when he returns home. He imagines kneeling before its wonders.

Dad drops Ricky at the airport, comes back to the silent closed-up house. The television is still off. He sets his keys on the kitchen table and moves to the bedroom where the head waits under its sheet. A blanket has come loose from the window, flooding the room with color. The alarm clock blinks with the wrong time, and in the moment between when he notices this and when he lifts off the sheet, he can't say what he dreads and what he hopes for, only that there is dread and hope overflowing in him, a terrible rise in heart rate, the brightness of the world turned up. He feels alive.

All this ringing energy rouses Foozie from her corner. She sits up and begins a slow, rhythmic barking.

Sullied Flesh
Karl Dandenell

Where to cross? Girard studied the traffic like a hunter in a blind, considering his options while warming his hands around a cup of extra-sweet cappuccino. Fuel-cell buses rolled by in stately procession, overtaken by faster hybrids and pure electric compacts. Every now and then, an exhaust-belching taxicab, blaring East Indian electronic trance music, cut across lanes in defiance of traffic laws and physics.

Jaywalking in New York wasn't illegal anymore, just dangerous.

He checked his watch, sipped coffee, and pondered the marquee across the street. RICHARD BURTON'S *HAMLET*, proclaimed the curved OLED screen above the box office. His jaw tightened. *It was Shakespeare's* Hamlet, *for Chrissakes.* After a moment, the screen grew dark, then revealed another message: STARRING GIRARD PETERSON. Girard nodded in quiet satisfaction. He'd done this play, wearing different NAGs, every season for his entire professional career. Union cards had their price.

But it was *wrong*. He was more than a meat puppet. And today he would prove it.

Girard screwed his courage to the sticking place and tugged

his wool cap down against the cold, damp November wind. With a quick inhalation, he kicked off like a sprinter, dodged a bike messenger, and hit the pavement next to the theater's rear exit. *Safe.* A passing driver cursed at him in Farsi. Girard automatically flipped them off. The door before him slammed open, and Angelo de Anda, the stage manager, burst out, eyes wild.

Right on cue. Angelo stood a head taller than him, a bearded giant who favored vintage business suits. He bought them at thrift stores, ripped out the charging cables and pocket humidors, and acid-washed them. He could easily pass as a victim of last decade's corporate downsizing.

Angelo's eyes locked with his. "Girard! What the *hell* is wrong with you?!" His voice threatened to crack, as it always did before a performance. The giant held up a bulky knockoff Rolex and violently pointed at it. "We are 46 minutes to curtain." He gulped air. "Forty. Six. Minutes. Barely enough time to dress, let alone—"

Girard held up a hand to forestall the rest. He finished his coffee in one long swallow to give himself time to find his center. "Dear Angelo, I'm *already* wearing my NAG." His voice was a near-perfect impression of Richard Burton's famous baritone. One hand tossed the empty coffee cup into a compost bin; the other doffed his wool cap. Under his short blond curls, his Neural Augmentation Gateway—his NAG—sat ready, a small band of flesh-colored biochips that filled the gap between his eyebrows and hairline. "Now, can we get inside? It's a witch's teat out here."

"Well, shit," Angelo said, and stood aside. Girard stepped past him, his body heavier, more solid with each step, more like a solid Welshman than a skinny kid named Jerry from Queens. "You're a *pendejo*, you know that?" the stage manager called at his back.

"Hamlet is the most royal of pains," replied Girard. He slipped inside the bathroom and locked the door behind him. Under the painfully bright fluorescent lights, he inspected the NAG. Angelo hadn't noticed anything, nor had Girard really expected him to. Still… he touched the warm plastic and scratched the skin near the edge, where it always itched. The NAG *looked* like the union model. It certainly irritated him like the real one.

"Be just and fear not," he told his reflection, and left the bathroom.

•

Actors filled the big unisex dressing room. Half sat before the wall mirror, checking their makeup. Others laced up doublets and bodices. Mike Chang, the new Bernardo, practiced his vocal exercises. "Ah-oh-ah-oh-hah!" The Best Nearly Broadway Theater's production of *Hamlet* ran four-and-a-half hours, and everyone tried to make the most of their prep time. Mike saw Girard enter the room and gave a quick wave. "Hi! Ho-hah!"

Girard waved back. He found the pre-curtain energy soothing, and he greeted people with nods and quick squeezes on the shoulder, working his way toward his locker.

Nancy Mishikawa, the company's tech, looked up from her datapad. "Not a great day to miss check-in," she said.

"We're losing our lease," said Mike.

"What?!"

"It's official," said Nancy, "the owner is selling. Yay, more condos."

"Oh shit." His mind flashed to the rest of the season. Would they be allowed to put on *Julius Caesar*, *The Crucible*, or even *The Foreigner*? *Shit. Shit. Shit.*

"It's not all bad news, though," Nancy continued. "I talked to the crew at the Orpheum and the Delacorte. They said Netflix reps were sniffing around both theaters last night. I'll bet we're next on their list."

Netflix was pouring a ton of money into programming, and that meant work. Even a small role in a series or movie would pay the rent for a long time. *And no NAGs.*

"I'll be with you as soon as I finish Alex." She waved the pad at Alexandria Nussbaum's NAG. Alex played Ophelia using the persona of Cate Blanchett. Her gateway was newer, smaller, and easier to hide in the actress's thick black hair. The biochip appliance was also—according to Nancy—fussy as a diva before an interview.

"Uh, sure," Girard said, opening his locker. Someone had plastered a giant red star decal on the scratched metal door and scribbled the words *This ego for rent* across the top. "Just give me a minute to slip into my finery and have some Irish courage."

Silence blossomed in the room, and several nearby actors took overt interest in their eye shadow, the lay of their ribbons, or the polish of a boot. Girard hung up his street clothes and slipped on his tights. As he rummaged around for his lucky socks, he felt something brush his temple. He turned slowly, found himself staring into Nancy's face. "Hello."

"Hello yourself," she said, and kissed him. "Just checking that you haven't spiked that evil coffee."

"Jeez, I was only kidding," he said, a bit louder than he'd intended. "I'm as sober as the Pope at Christmas, I swear." Behind them, someone let loose a nervous laugh.

The first time he'd put on the Burton NAG, he'd fallen so far into the actor's persona that he'd shown up drunk at rehearsal. Fortunately, the director had chosen to blame the NAG programmer and not Girard's lack of self-control. Since that day, Girard had used meditation and breathing exercises to keep his identity strictly separate from the artificial persona.

"Just wanted to make sure." Nancy leaned in further and whispered, "I bought some new massage oil. We can test drive it after the show."

Blood rose to his cheeks. "Anything you say. Now let me get dressed, wench."

She ran fingers over his eyebrows. "You know, I don't care if your roommate was top of his class at MIT. If he synched your NAG wrong and it hiccups during a soliloquy, *I'm* responsible." She wrapped fingers around a blond curl and tugged it, hard. "They could *yank* my union card. That's not going to happen, is it?"

"Perish the thought," Girard replied through clenched teeth.

"That's my boy." Nancy released him. "Break a leg, everybody!" She packed up her gear and left.

Girard turned and gave the actors a wide grin. "It's show time!"

•

"Whither wilt thou lead me? Speak; I'll go no further." Girard stopped pacing across the stage, leaned back, and fought the impulse to cross his arms. Harry Sanchez faced him. The old character actor's stylized armor, bathed in a nimbus of holographic fog, transformed him into the somber ghost of Hamlet's father.

"Mark me!" cried the ghost in the rafter-shaking tones of Brian Blessed.

"I will." Girard's voice was quiet in comparison, echoes of a child who has recently lost a parent.

"My hour is almost come, when I to sulf'rous and tormenting flames must render up myself." The ghost's eyes clouded over in anticipation of his coming pain.

"Alas, poor ghost."

"Pity me not, but lend thy serious hearing to what I shall unfold."

"Speak. I am bound to hear." Girard stepped closer, his sense of duty overcoming his fear of this apparition.

The ghost drew himself up taller, regaining a measure of his former vitality. "So art thou to revenge, when thou shalt hear."

Girard had scanned the audience from the wings during the first scene. There were no obvious agents with their oh-so-trendy leather coats, but he'd marked plenty of students, couples, fellow actors, and Valerie D., the caustic reviewer from the *City Curmudgeon.com*. She was sitting in the second row, dead center. Her Holographic Activity Gatherer, onyx-black, blinked slowly, like a traffic warning. Valerie's eyes had the telltale look of the HAG-ridden. The thousand-yard stare, as Girard's grandfather used to say.

After the show, the reviewer would download her memories to her laptop and edit her opinions—Girard suspected—using the style of Joan Didion, Oscar Wilde, or maybe even Kurt Vonnegut. Heaven forbid she try anything *original*, like her own voice.

But Girard reminded himself that a bad review was the least of his worries tonight, for time was out of joint.

Across the stage, the ghost continued his complaints.

•

Later, Girard stood in the wings and absentmindedly rubbed his forehead while Polonius and his servant awaited Ophelia. Girard's budding headache was more than the NAG; it was anxiety sinking its teeth into his neck. For three months, while his roommate Migdad had reverse-engineered the NAG, Girard had honed his Burton doppelgänger. Now that the night had arrived, he wasn't as confident as he'd hoped.

He squeezed an acupressure point between his thumb and forefinger, wondering if they should have run more tests. The Richard Burton persona overlay had been assembled from old film footage, interviews, and interpretations by a dozen directors. It wasn't an exact copy, which was why Girard had chosen it. Burton's spirits filled his bones, but the meat was all him. Would it be enough?

•

"What are people thinking?" his grandfather Joe had asked Girard over a couple of rum and Cokes during last summer's record heat wave. It was 110 degrees in the shade, and no one felt like moving.

"When NATO dumped combat training into people's brains before the Iran shit, everybody screamed 'Frankenstein.' Now you're telling me that you *have* to wear a NAG to get a theater job? Kee-christ." Joe wiped his sweaty forehead with a faded cotton handkerchief. "I just don't get it."

"Consumer NAGs are different," Girard had said patiently. They'd had this discussion before, but the old man had difficulty recalling their previous talks. Despite targeted gene therapy, Alzheimer's still stalked him. "The biochips aren't as powerful. I'm not a robot. Really." God, was he whining?

"Uh, huh. What if the program wants you to say something you don't like?"

"Well." Girard paused. "Some NAG programs are more tightly written than others. If you license Cumberbatch's *Macbeth*, you have to do the whole thing verbatim." He added quickly, "But that's not the case with every show."

"I bet it is with the popular ones," his grandfather said with the confidence of age. "It's going to be Disney all over again."

Girard drank his rum and Coke in silence.

•

After he killed Polonius, Hamlet sat on the Queen's bed and calmly continued their conversation. Girard's head pounded, and his NAG kept prodding him to stand, to pace, to cry out his lines in Burton-ish fashion. Wrong, it felt wrong. Too easy to rail against the heavens and play the madman. Wasn't there greater power in quiet madness, to use this moment of shared horror to try to connect one last time with his mother? He decided to risk it.

The Queen clutched her hands, imploring, "What shall I do?"

Girard closed his eyes as if considering his answer and triggered the interrupt switch in his NAG. Half a breath later, the mask of Richard Burton fell away, and Girard continued with only the barest of flutters in his stomach. "Not this, by no means, that I bid you do…" He reached out to touch the Queen's cheek, hesitated, drew back, then forged ahead. When he spoke of going to England, it was with true sadness. He didn't want to leave his mother now, not when she needed him! Yet he had a duty. With a sad smile, he pulled back the arras again and made to pick up the body within. "Good night, Mother."

The Queen gathered up her dignity and exited stage right. Girard glanced after her, nodded, and grabbed Polonius' doublet. He dragged the body out, a grim smile on his face.

•

Girard always loved the fourth act. The actors playing Rosencrantz and Guildenstern were old friends; they had all performed *Rosencrantz and Guildenstern are Dead* together during their time at SUNY. Their familiar energy and japes gave Girard a much-needed boost, and he once again cast aside Burton's mask to muse on the impending death of twenty thousand men. Resolved to his own bloody thoughts, he exited stage left, where Nancy waited.

"Hey," she whispered. Horatio, Gertrude, and a Gentleman entered from stage right.

"Hey yourself," Girard whispered back.

"How're you holding up?" she asked, and leaned in for a

quick kiss. He returned the kiss, added a wink.

"High and tight."

"That's good," she said. "The director thinks you're extra cocky tonight. He's worried you're overshadowing Claudius again."

Girard rolled his eyes. "That's my *job*. Besides, what do they expect with Patrick Stewart's NAG?"

"Yeah," said Nancy, nodding. "I always thought his Claudius was a bit prissy."

"The first time I saw him hand over the poisoned wine, I expected him to say 'Engage!'"

Nancy chuckled quietly. Then, tiptoeing closer to the curtain, she listened to the dialog and checked her watch. "Almost time, Jerry."

"I know."

She gave him an appraising look. "Seriously… are you okay?"

"Tell the director I'm fine."

"I will, but something's off. Some of the other actors think you're channeling Burton's ego again."

More often than not, Nancy knew when he was hiding something. Girard casually brushed at his hair. "Just a bigger headache than usual," he said with reassuring casualness. "We all suffer for our art."

"Now you know how I feel about high heels." She studied him for another moment. Finally, she whispered, "Time," and bounded off, a gazelle in a concrete savannah.

Girard squared his shoulders, took a deep breath, and switched on the NAG. He'd let Burton's ghost out to play for now.

•

Laertes leapt into the grave and commanded to be buried with his sister. Hamlet broke from his hiding place and announced himself. "What is he whose grief bears such an emphasis, whose phrase of sorrow conjures the wand'ring stars, and makes them stand like wonder-wounded heroes? This is I, Hamlet the Dane."

"The devil take thy soul!" cried Laertes, and pulled the prince into the grave. Hamlet landed on his knees, then commanded Laertes to hold off his hand.

They wrestled while the Queen called her son's name and the funeral attendants swarmed forward to separate them. One attendant missed his blocking and grabbed Hamlet by his collar rather than his shoulder. Girard twisted to the side to compensate, and smacked his head into the aluminum and plywood grave painted to look like soil. He felt a corner of the NAG scrape off. Instantly, Burton's ghost fled. Girard's head throbbed.

"Good my lord, be quiet," said Horatio, both stern and compassionate.

Girard pressed the NAG back down against his forehead. Nothing. He conjured the NAG's password. Nothing. *Oh shit.*

Sensing a problem, the Queen stepped toward him, waited a beat, then spoke her line: "O my son, what theme?"

Girard dropped his hands. "I loved Ophelia. Forty thousand brothers could not make up my sum. What wilt thou do for her?" He stared at Laertes, wincing internally over the botched line.

"O," the King said, "he is mad, Laertes." He was gentle, almost fatherly.

"For the love of God forebear him," the Queen said.

"'Swounds, show me what thou't do," Girard said. He pushed away the men who stood near him and clenched his fists. The old somatic worked, and he remembered: "Woo't weep? Woo't fight? Woo't fast?" The words came more smoothly now, and he let his arms drop.

Somehow Girard finished the scene, offering up a quick prayer of thanks to whatever gods watched over actors and fools as he and Horatio exited stage right. During the scenery change, Nancy pounced on him. "What the hell?" She sealed the NAG down with makeup adhesive. Girard tried to help but Nancy slapped his hands away. "Let me do it."

"I'm okay," he hissed.

"Is it online?"

"Signal cut out when I hit my head."

"Shit. We'll have to go to intermission while I get the backup."

"Don't," Girard insisted. "*Please*, Nancy, it'll throw off the whole show if we stop now."

Nancy glanced behind him, saw Horatio waiting under the Elsinor holograph, pleading with his eyes. "Goddamit. I *knew* you were up to something." She grabbed Girard's shoulders with painful strength. "If you miss one more line, I'll drop the curtain on your ass."

"I can *do* this, I swear."

She pushed him toward the waiting Horatio. "Prove it."

•

Laertes and Girard stood facing each other, sweating, trying not to pant. Their swords did not waver. The Queen clutched a cloth to her pale forehead.

"Come, for the third, Laertes: you do but dally," Girard said. He had flustered his opponent and it showed in the other's sloppy blade work. "I pray you pass with your best violence; I am afeared you make a wanton of me."

Laertes straightened and glared. "Say you so? Come on!" He launched a feint toward Girard's chest, then dropped the point at the last moment, hoping to score a touch above the knee. Girard beat in eight, and riposted. Laertes retreated, cutting the air with his blade.

Girard drew his left foot forward in preparation to lunge. At the last moment, Laertes seemed to notice this and counterattacked with a stop thrust. Girard beat back, feinted, thrust.

Osric, looking on, stopped the action and declared no legal touch.

Laertes lost his temper. "Have at you now!" he shouted and leapt forward. They grappled corps-a-corps, dropping their weapons. Girard snatched up Laertes' blade and stabbed the other man in the shoulder.

"Part them. They are incensed," said Claudius.

"Nay, come—again!" cried Girard. He started toward his opponent as the Queen collapsed.

"Look to the queen there, ho!"

Moments later, the Queen fell, poisoned.

"O villainy! Ho! Let the door be locked! Treachery! Seek it out."

Laertes fell, and confessed.

Girard stabbed the King, then begged the poisoned cup from Horatio.

"O, I die, Horatio! The potent poison quite o'ercrows my spirit. I cannot live to hear the news from England, but I do prophesy th' election lights on Fortinbras. He has my dying voice." He raised his hand to clutch his friend's shoulder. "So tell him, with th' occurrents, more and less, which have solicited—the rest is silence."

He slipped gratefully to the stage.

•

After the curtain calls, Girard hastily dressed and stole away to a nearby cafe, where he parked himself in a corner with a tray of demitasse cups, sweets, and his phone. He didn't want to be around the company, knowing that he'd either have to confess his scheme or serve up some serious bullshit that might or might not work.

Just as Girard had finished reviewing all the open casting calls, Nancy strode in, wearing an enormous fur coat of questionable ancestry. She blinked, her eyes adjusting to the dim interior light, then spotted Girard. With enviable grace, she negotiated a pathway between tables, easing into the vacant chair next to him.

"How did you know I'd be here?" Girard said.

"This is where we had our first breakfast together," she replied. "It's your happy place."

"I guess it is," he said. "Want some coffee?"

"*Yuck.*" She grimaced and pulled back her coat to reveal a

silver whiskey flask tucked into a nylon holster that occasionally housed a 9mm SIG Sauer. "I was thinking you might need something stronger."

"God, yes," Girard said. "You are an angel."

"Only when I want to be." Nancy nabbed two clean water glasses from a nearby table and poured a couple of fingers of whiskey into them. She knocked her own back, refilled it. Then she produced Girard's NAG from her pocket. "This is broken, by the way."

Girard took the NAG. "Well, shit. I'll have to use the backup and get this one fixed."

"Yeah, about that," Nancy said. "There's a biochip in there that doesn't match the others. An interrupt? Something your roommate printed in your basement?"

"At his lab," Girard admitted.

"Jesus. He probably broke half a dozen IP laws," she said.

"I didn't ask."

"And how long have you been faking it?" Nancy asked.

"I've never faked it."

"Asshole."

"Sorry," Girard said. "Not that long. A few weeks, maybe a month." *Or two.* "I started cutting off the persona a few minutes at a time. Minor speeches, stuff like that. Then, when no one noticed..." He tapped the NAG against the table. "This is the fake, Nancy. This—" he pointed at his heart and dropped his voice into Burton's register— "this is real. Living flesh and blood, complete with mistakes and foibles, not some bit-copy of an actor's better days."

"Well I hope it's worth losing your union card," she replied, taking another shot.

"Are you going to turn me in?" Girard said, shifting back to his own voice.

Nancy drew his hand up and nipped at his knuckles. "Not at the moment."

"*Thank you.*" His shoulders relaxed. A little.

"Don't thank me yet. You're going to write a confession that clearly states you acted on your own. I'll keep a copy in case you do something stupid." She released Girard's hand. "Have to look out for my best interests, after all."

"Of course," Girard said, and leaned over for a kiss. Nancy put a hand up, catching him under the sternum.

"Jerry, I like you a lot, and you have some real talent. But this is crap." She moved his hand up and cupped his chin. "If you want to do live theater, then *do* it." She squeezed his jaw. "Don't dick around with the tourists who think they're seeing Burton. Let 'em watch *Beckett* on TV if they want that."

"Understood."

"And don't lie to me ever again. I'm a big girl, and if I don't like what I hear, I can handle it."

"I *am* sorry about that. Truly."

"As you should be," she said, letting him go.

He leaned back. "Nancy, when I was in college, hardly anybody could afford NAGs. There were just two theater companies using them. Today, there are four productions of Hamlet, and all of them use NAGs." He counted on his fingers. "You have your choice of Ken Branagh, Benedict Cumberbatch,

David Tenant, or Richard Burton. So what makes us special?

"They come to see *me*, not some puppet dancing to the strings of a dead actor. And every night, it's different. They see inspiration, love, struggle—"

"Clumsiness," said Nancy.

"And clumsiness," he agreed. "That's what makes it unique. That moment will never be repeated." He took a drink. "At least I hope it won't."

"Even if you do, you'll manage."

"Thanks."

"Seriously, Jerry. You did okay tonight, all things considered."

"Just okay?"

"Okay, you had some *really* good moments, at least according to Luis Carrasco."

"Wait. The artistic director from Bard Without a Net?"

"That's the guy," said Nancy. "He was talking to some of the cast in the vaping area after the show. They're having invite-only auditions next week." She bumped her phone to Gerard's. "And you're invited."

Girard glanced down at the calendar link flashing on his screen. "Huh."

"I think the phrase you're looking for is 'Thank you.'"

"Thank you!" Bard Without a Net specialized in minimal staging and costumes, with cast members taking on a different role every night based on a random number generator. It wasn't Netflix-level money, but it was something. "It would be a real challenge."

"More challenging than pretending you're a dead guy?" said Nancy. "Come on, get real."

Girard held her eyes for an awkward moment, measuring his words and courage. She was right. If he was going to do this, he had to do it. "'Arm me, audacity, from head to foot!'" he said.

"Come again?"

"I will swallow my fear and offer a proper *mea culpa* for the cast and the director first thing tomorrow."

"Wise decision," said Nancy. Then she made an overly casual gesture of looking at her watch. "Now, I think I mentioned something about a massage."

Girard stood and offered his hand. "Yes, ma'am."

"Me first," she said. "And don't forget the feet."

"Perish the thought."

The Selkie Wife
Marcie Lynn Tentchoff

She would not say farewell,
only that the spell was broken.
She drew a tangled ball of sealskin
from her dresser,
and then,
before the sun was fully risen,
sought her exit through
a rainbow tinted puddle
spilled on their front drive.
Behind her, he stood
stoking his confusion
with his store of twisted memories,
glossing over words he'd spoken,
names he'd called her,
all his jealousy of her magic gifts
as bitter as the tea
that she'd left slowly brewing,
steeping, strengthening,
simmering upon the stove.

The Edge of Galaxy NGC 4013
Warren Brown

I saw the edge
Of 4013
In email color

Hi thirty-two bit
Creation's gift
Right there

On the screen
It sang out
In light

I was pixilated
Transformed
Amid coffee
And work papers

The detritus
Of employment
The detritus

Of stars

Heart singing
I flew
From the mundane
And back

Shaking off
The impossible
Cold of space

I shimmered
Like star stuff

Picked up a pen
And wrote
This love note
To God

After Dinner Conversation: An Interview with Publisher Kolby Granville

David F. Shultz and Kolby Granville

DFS: Before we go into the deeper discussion, could you talk a bit about *After Dinner Conversation*? What kind of stories do you publish, and what is your editorial vision in a nutshell?

KG: We publish short fictional stories, of any genre, so long as they ask interesting ethical or philosophical questions. From a writing standpoint, think of "The Ones Who Walk Away From Omelas," "Harrison Burgeron," or "Flowers for Algernon." We really don't care about the genre, so long as there is a deeper universal question to discuss.

DFS: *After Dinner Conversation* has a cross-media approach to content delivery. Can you talk about your publication model, and how new media platforms can change the way people engage with stories?

KG: Right now, each story is published as a digital single, as part of a monthly magazine, and as a print anthology. Many of the stories are also discussed in our podcast. We like to think that we aren't simply publishing a story, but rather promoting a mission, the mission of getting people to have thoughtful conversations. It just so happens we do that by publishing stories. At some point we would like to have a print version of the magazine, but at this point it just doesn't seem like it's worth it for the cost and effort that would be involved, but who knows what the future may hold.

DFS: You're looking for stories that can serve as thought experiments or platforms for further discussion. How big is the *ADC* collection now, and what kind of issues have you explored so far?

KG: We are looking for stories that touch on "universal questions" or "universal truths." It should be the kind of story where, if you read it 100 years from now, the themes are still relevant. So, for example, we had an author submit a story that named Donald Trump by name and it was very topical. There is nothing wrong with sending us a story about the nature of leadership, the nature of power, or the nature of the risks in how governments structure themselves, but we really didn't want to write a story that was about Donald Trump. We asked the writer to change the story just a bit to remove the specific names and identifying features, and focus on the universality of the themes.

We have 75 short stories that have been accepted. We have two paperback anthologies that are out, with a third on the way. We also are six months into our monthly magazine. As a general rule, we shoot for one new short story every week.

DFS: Ethical issues are a natural fit for fiction, because moral dilemmas lead to dramatic conflict; but to what extent does ADC explore other branches of philosophy, like metaphysics, epistemology, or aesthetics?

KG: Yes. We have, or want to explore, every aspect of philosophy. Of course some, like theory of perception or utility are easier to write and think about, but we are very interested in every area. For us, a good story starts with the question being asked, and the author would work backwards from the question to come up with a scenario to explore that question.

DFS: I know you're open to any genre—provided it poses the right kind of questions—but since *Speculative North* is an SFF magazine, I was interested in your view of speculative fiction. Are there sorts of questions that are more common in SFF? Have you noticed that SFF has any particular strengths or weaknesses for engaging with philosophical issues?

KG: We get a lot of SFF submissions. I think that it has, historically, lent itself to these sorts of morality plays, at least the best of it does. It's also very easy to set up unique situations. Really, all you have to say is, "In another world where…" and you can set up any sort of hypothetical you want. And we are fine with that. Star Trek was really great at doing this. They land on a new planet, and the people have a special trait that allows a unique question to be asked. It's never about the plot, for us; it's about the question the plot allows us to explore.

That said, we would love to get submissions of other genres that ask interesting questions. We have never gotten a romance submission, a western submission, or a noir style submission and we would love to. We just haven't gotten any!

DFS: Besides the obvious and general reasons stories get rejected, like not following guidelines or not keeping reader interest, are there other big reasons that otherwise good stories don't make the cut for ADC?

KG: I initially assumed that the main reason we would turn down stories would be based on the quality of the writing, but because the publication is so unique, the biggest reason for turning things down is that it doesn't fit what we do. We have a form letter for stories that aren't a good fit (because we have to send it so many times); we don't have a form for stories that are not well written-- there aren't enough of these to warrant a form. People assume that "all genres" means anything goes; while we take everything, we really have a very narrow focus, like our own genre.

DFS: What's the quickest way for a writer to grab your interest from the *ADC* slushpile?

KG: This is going to sound weird to say, but while quality of writing is important, that's not the key to getting published. 80% of the writing we get is of "good enough" or better writing quality. Really, the fastest way is to get published with us is to come up with an idea that's new.

For example, the story that won our writing contest recently-- "waiting room" opens with three people in a waiting room, waiting to be assigned new "life dreams" by the government. Three sentences in and we knew if the writing held up, and there was a competent ending, we were going to publish it.

DFS: Do you see a lot of didactic or preachy stories in the slushpile? How can an author avoid falling into that trap?

KG: I would say 1 in 5 stories fall into that category. Sometimes the question asked is so obvious, and the answer is so easy, it's just not a useful story for us. Questions should move to something bigger; like the changing values in a society, or disagreements about moral boundaries, or generational views on ethics—questions where there are ideas, but not definitive conclusions.

DFS: Some of your stories cover sensitive and politically charged issues. Have any stories created inadvertent pushback or offense from readers? Should authors approach these issues in any particular way to prevent controversy, or manage how the story will be received?

KG: Write your truth. That's rule #1. If you don't write your truth, it really doesn't matter what you are writing, or how well you are writing it. I'm sure a few authors have thought we rejected their stories because they were too risky or too edgy, but I can assure you, that has never been the case, at least with us. I'm not saying there are no boundaries, but we haven't found them yet.

DFS: Are there any positive reactions from readers and listeners that really stood out to you? Do you like connecting with fans, and is there a good way that they can reach out to you?

KG: We have gotten some really wonderful letters from readers. The ones that stick with me the most are the ones where parents use the stories as a tool to talk to and learn about the opinions of their teenage children. It's interesting how much time you can spend with your child without ever really having a deeper conversation with them. Our stories make that process easier to do. We usually get emails, which we are thrilled to get at editor@afterdinnerconversation.com

DFS: What's the best way people can support *After Dinner Conversation?*

KG: Of course, we would love it if people would support us on Patreon, or subscribe to the monthly magazine. Money is always an issue for independent magazines, and it is with us as well. That said, just reading the stories, sharing them with friends, and extending our mission is wonderful as well.

•

Kolby Granville is the founder and editor-in-chief at *After Dinner Conversation*. He is a former humanities teacher as well as a recovering lawyer and city council member. He loves ethics, philosophy, economics, and political theory. Even if he knew what it did, he would eat the apple anyway. In his free time he is a movie and travel junkie. His favorite authors are Kurt Vonnegut, Chuck Palahniuk, Joss Whedon, Aristotle, and Thomas Jefferson.

The *After Dinner Conversation* short stories, magazine, and associated podcast series can be found online at afterdinnerconversation.com.

Craft: The Narrative Lens
David F. Shultz

Writers don't describe. That's a painter's job. Writers render experiences by filtering them through a narrative lens.

Is the cigar smoke "coiled around her neck" or "draped over her shoulders"? Nothing in the physical scene determines this.

"How do you describe a werewolf?" is not the question; "How does the protagonist see a werewolf?" is the question. The answer is: it depends on whether they are a werewolf-hunter or someone trying to run away.

A sad person might see the gray clouds, and a happy person might see the bright sun, looking up at the same sky. Our mindset and personality shapes what we perceive, so your character's mindset should shape your narrative.

A scene cannot be described without knowing who is telling the story, or what kind of story it is meant to be. To properly render a scene, you need a narrative lens.

The Narrative Lens

The narrative lens comprises all the high-level, structural considerations that can be brought to bear on word choice when rendering a scene. The most important considerations are about your point of view character: what sort of things do they notice;

what kind of language do they use; do they have habits of thought; are they in a particular mood; etc. The narrative lens also includes other high-level considerations in story construction: establishing tone, developing theme or motif, foreshadowing. However, these should be secondary to considerations of the point of view character; theme, motif, and foreshadowing should emerge organically, as much as possible, from the narration, which strives primarily for psychological fidelity.

You cannot properly render a scene or describe something in a story unless you figure out (or intuitively appreciate) the narrative lens for that scene. Even in scenes without a point of view character, in scenes with distant or omniscient narrators, and in scenes with no characters at all, description is filtered through a narrative lens. In these cases, the narrative lens is more abstract—comprising structural and thematic considerations, without the psychological leaning of the POV character—but it is still there.

The narrative lens can be thought of as an aspect of point of view. People often think of point of view in terms of person and tense. A story is told from a particular vantage point, thus there are limitations on the pronouns and tenses that are used to describe events, and deviation from those rules can constitute a point of view error. The narrative lens provides similar, though softer and subtler, constraints. An easy example is diction. Consider a medieval fantasy story with an omniscient third-person narrator, in which there is no central character; though the narrator is an abstraction, it would still feel wrong for the narration to contain modern terms or neologisms, such as describing a soaring dragon as a "green 747", or an army of mercenary knights as being funded through "crowdsourcing". Modern terms are inappropriate because they are outside of the narrative lens for this kind of story (an exception would be deliberately using this inconsistency for humour—in this case, "comedy" is part of the narrative lens). Likewise, word choices can feel tonally or thematically inappropriate, depending on whether the story is a romance, a comedy, or a horror. In all cases, description can feel "off" to the extent that it falls outside of the narrative lens.

The narrative lens is constructed in the mind of the reader while they take in the story. In most cases, the reader very quickly learns the tense and person of the story. But other aspects of the narrative lens are often built more slowly and by degrees. Parts of the POV character come to be revealed—maybe age, level of education, profession—all of which shape the narrative lens and so should affect the descriptions subsequently deployed. And there are aspects of the broader story that come to be revealed— the tone, the theme, the setting. The narrative lens is simultaneously a product of the text and a constraint on the text, existing as a literary abstraction.

Just as picking words outside of the narrative lens can feel wrong, picking words in its center can create evocative effects. In a well-written story, word choices and sentence constructions bend towards the narrative lens, allowing the reader to feel its presence without explication. This technique is a form of "show, don't tell". While we could explicitly state that a character is sad ("telling"), we might more artfully omit this explicit statement and instead simply describe their perception in a way that creates a felt presence of their sadness. A sad character's text is different from a happy character's text; effective narration reflects differences in mindset. By rendering description in accordance with a character's narrative lens, the reader can be made to feel the lens's presence (e.g. "sadness") without being explicitly told.

Bottom-line: The narrative lens is critical to prose fiction. Every story has a narrative lens, which is simultaneously a product of the text and a constraint on the text. You cannot properly describe a scene without a narrative lens.

Exercises

These exercises are meant to practice the skill of narrative lensing. Some of these you will find easier than others. Some of them will seem very strange. Between the whole set, they cover a wide variety of different sources of narrative lensing: tone, emotional context, psychological disposition, expertise, diction, etc.

For each of the following exercises, there is a scene to describe, and a narrative lens. Your job is to use the narrative lens to render the scene. Don't take too long on these; it's mostly about picking a few details and choosing how to present them. Remember: the whole point is seeing how the narrative lens shapes the description.

General instructions:
- use about 2 to 5 sentences per description exercise
- spend no more than 4 minutes per exercise
- focus on sensory details and experiences; try to hit 3 senses

per exercise

- "show" rather than "tell" the prompt

<u>Exercises:</u>

1. Describe a pub, from the POV of a trained assassin who suspects someone is trying to kill him.
2. Describe a pub, from the POV of a recovering alcoholic who is there to meet an old friend.
3. Describe a ballroom, from the POV of an undercover agent who is posing as a wealthy investor as part of an investigation.
4. Describe a grocery store, from the POV of a shopper whose family has recently died in a plane crash.
5. Describe a grocery store, from the POV of someone who has recently won the lottery.
6. Describe a fist fight, witnessed from the POV of a music teacher who has never been in a fight.
7. Describe a fist fight, witnessed from the POV of a retired boxer.
8. Describe the steps to the courthouse, from the POV of a paraplegic ex-marine.
9. Describe a sky-dive, from the POV of someone obsessed with collecting marbles.
10. Describe a presidential speech, from the POV of a child who wants ice cream.
11. Describe a presidential speech, from the POV of someone with blackmail material against the president.
12. Describe a presidential speech, from the POV of an alien

who has come to Earth in human form to investigate our society.

13. Describe an old/malfunctioning starship engine from the POV of an expert starship mechanic.

14. Describe an old/malfunctioning car engine from the point of view of an expert mechanic.

15. Describe a scroll of spells that was recently discovered, from the POV of an expert wizard.

16. Describe a wall of hieroglyphics that was recently discovered, from the POV of an expert archaeologist.

17. Describe a delivery van, in an early scene in a horror story about a gang that kills people to sell body parts.

18. Describe a funeral home, in a scene during the second act of a comedy about college students experimenting with drugs for their blog.

19. Describe a train station, from the POV of a blind person.

20. Describe an airport, using a third-person omniscient POV, in a story about how people around the world are affected by the world coming to an end because of a climate catastrophe.

21. Describe the planet Jupiter, using a third-person omniscient POV, in a story about the pioneers and scientists involved in humankind's colonization of other planets.

Response from Y.M. Pang

Not much to add here, except that I agree. A scene consists of who is telling it as much as what happens in it.

That being said, I encourage writers to think of narrative lensing as a way to enhance their writing, rather than a way to restrict it. It's not a ship to tie your novel to (and potentially sink on). There are times when writing the scene exactly as your character would see it would be untenable, or create more problems than it solves.

Perhaps there is a certain detail about a room that the average person wouldn't notice, so maybe it isn't entirely realistic that one of your characters notices. Maybe you are switching to the point of view of a child, and writing a scene exactly as a child would see it might be too jarring compared to the rest of the book, or would sound too juvenile for a target audience that is not intended to be children. Perhaps, as David mentioned, there are themes, motifs, or foreshadowing to be established; I agree those are secondary to conveying characterization, but they are considerations nonetheless.

A story, especially if it is in third person, does not need to be a perfect representation of everything the character senses and feels and absolutely nothing of what they are less likely to sense and feel. There can be a certain amount of balance with other narrative considerations, as long as the writing isn't blatantly ignoring what the POV character would be sensing. Don't make the most absent-minded character the one who notices the detail in the room (unless there is a reason they were triggered into awareness). Don't have a character cracking jokes in their head right after their best friend died (unless this is a particularly morbid character). Do not, in other words, stray so far out from the point of view that the reader notices it—and either flags it as an error or grossly misunderstands the character.

The narrative lens doesn't need to be realistic—but it needs to be believable. As much as possible, strive to convey the unique way this character looks at the world. However, if you find yourself rewriting half the book because you're not sure whether the POV character should've noticed the colour of the vase, then you've probably gone too far.

Conveying each character's unique way of interacting with the world is also an excellent tool when writing multiple POVs in the same story. It can really help distinguish voices, personalities, and stages in life, without resorting to "telling." However, this too can be a balancing act. Some writers prefer employing a vastly different narrative lens for each POV, even changing writing styles or narrative voice when switching. This can be effective at conveying (and inciting) a wide range of emotions, and also demonstrates a writer's versatility. Many other writers, however, find such a method jarring within a single story and prone to calling too much attention to itself. These writers prefer keeping a similar style throughout while conveying different POVs in more subtle ways. There is no single right way to do this. Where to land on the scale depends on the specific story, and the type of reading experience you wish to give to your audience.

In light of this, I would like to offer an additional writing exercise (as if David hadn't given enough homework already!). It's good practice to write all those varied characters, but I'm sure you want to write your own characters better. So: Take three characters from your own story. This could be your work in progress, or even a story still in the planning stages, as long as all three characters come from the same story. Put those characters in one of the settings listed in David's writing prompts: an airport, a starship, an ancient tomb covered in hieroglyphics—your pick. Write a scene for each of them in that setting. Though they are in the exact same setting, convey how each of them sees it differently.

Then: Take the protagonists from three of your stories. Three different stories. Repeat this exercise.

Good luck, and happy writing.

—Y.M. Pang

Y.M. Pang is a Toronto-based author whose fiction has appeared in *The Magazine of Fantasy & Science Fiction*, *Strange Horizons*, *Clarkesworld*, and many other venues. She is a Submissions Editor with *Speculative North*, and a dabbler in photography and art.

About the Contributors

Warren Brown
Author, "The Edge of Galaxy NGC 4013"
Warren Brown is a dual Canadian/American citizen and currently lives and writes fiction and poetry in Tulsa OK, with his wife Lana Brown, also a writer. He has published fiction in *OMNI*, *F&SF*, *Amazing* and other magazines, and poetry in *This Land*, *Nimrod*, *Dear Leader Tales*, etc. His novel, *What Happened in Fool the Eye* is available on Amazon, Barnes and Noble, and Smashwords websites.
http://warrenbrown.synthasite.com/

Kai Calo
Author, "The Vulture Man"
Kai Calo loves animals, aliens, and horror. She's a fan of anything with a dark or disturbing element. She doesn't like bios that much. Among her influences are authors Ursula K. Le Guin, Victor Hugo, Cormac McCarthy, and Clive Barker. She is an active member of the Horror Writers Association as well as the Florida Writers Association. She currently lives in Florida with her cats.
www.kaicalo.com

Karl Dandenell
Author, "Sullied Flesh"
Karl Dandenell is an Active Member of the Science Fiction Writers of America who lives on an island near San Francisco with his family and cat overlords. He is fond of strong tea,

distilled spirits, and British crime dramas. When not editing help files for a major healthcare organization, he reads a lot of speculative fiction, and serves as a First Reader for *The Magazine of Fantasy & Science Fiction*.

Find him at www.firewombats.com or on Twitter @Kdandenell.

Andy Dibble
Author, "Bang the Drum"
Andy Dibble is a former academic and Sanskritist turned healthcare IT consultant. He lives near his hometown in southern Wisconsin, but has supported the electronic medical record of large healthcare systems in six countries. His work also appears or is forthcoming in *Writers of the Future, Sci Phi Journal, Star*Line*, and others. You can find him at andydibble.com.

Eran Fowler
Artist, "Noctua Steal the Moon"
Eran Fowler is an illustrator currently residing in BC, Canada. Eran has always been interested in the storytelling possibilities of visual art, and feels most at home using magical realism to explore what it means to be human.
Website: http://eranfolio.com/

Brian Koukol
Author, "Autumn in the Dying Light"
Brian Koukol, raised in the suburbs of Los Angeles, now makes his home among the salt breezes and open spaces of California's Central Coast. A lifelong battle with muscular dystrophy has informed the majority of his work, which is written with the aid of voice recognition software out of necessity. His words have appeared in *Phantaxis Magazine, GigaNotoSaurus,* and *The Baltimore Review*, amongst other places.
Website: www.briankoukol.com, Twitter: @BrianKoukol

Rudy Kremberg
Author, "The Air Show"
Rudy Kremberg is a Toronto-based writer whose fiction has appeared in genre magazines (e.g., *Interzone*), literary journals (e.g., *Queen's Quarterly*), anthologies and various other venues, ranging from *Storyteller* to *The Tampa Tribune* to *Knave*. His work has also been adapted for television (the horror series *The Hunger*) and broadcast on CBC Radio. His most recent publications are short stories in *Shadowy Natures*, an anthology from Dark Ink, and *BFS Horizons*, the British Fantasy Society's fiction magazine. His nonfiction credits include articles in consumer magazines and trade periodicals, covering topics as diverse as medical research and gourmet cheese. "The Air Show" is a revised version of a story that originally appeared in the June 2015 issue of *Disturbed Digest*.

Eric Lewis
Author, "The Heron King"
By day Eric Lewis is a research scientist weathering the latest rounds of mergers and layoffs and trying to remember how to be a person again after surviving grad school. His short fiction has been published in *Nature, Cossmass Infinities, Electric Spec, Bards & Sages Quarterly*, the anthologies *Crash Code, Into Darkness Peering* and *Best Indie Speculative Fiction Vol. 1*, the short story collection *Tricks of the Blade* as well as other venues detailed at ericlewis.ink. His debut novel *The Heron Kings* is available from Flame Tree Press.

Christi Nogle
Author, "The Laffun Head"
Christi Nogle's most recent stories appear in *Three-lobed Burning Eye, PseudoPod, Hermine Annual*, and *Fusion Fragment*. Christi teaches English at Boise State University and lives in Boise with

her partner Jim and their gorgeous dogs. Follow her at christinogle.com or on Twitter @christinogle

Marcie Lynn Tentchoff
Author, "The Selkie Wife"
Marcie Lynn Tentchoff is a poet/writer/editor from the west coast of Canada, where she lives surrounded by dense forest and less dense creatures, some of whom are her family. Her work has appeared in such publications as *On Spec*, *Star*Line*, and *Strange Horizons*.